# CAST IRON

*Julia McAllister Mysteries*
*Book Two*

## Marilyn Todd

SAPERE
BOOKS

# CAST IRON

Published by Sapere Books.

20 Windermere Drive, Leeds, England, LS17 7UZ,
United Kingdom

saperebooks.com

ISBN: 978-1-913335-03-8

*For Janet and Richard —*
*Friends are like stars.*
*You don't always see 'em — but they're there!*

# Chapter 1

4.30... 4.30... The time rattled in her head like wheels over the rails. 4.30 and then, with a piercing whistle and a cloud of white steam, the train would chug out of the station, taking Julia McAllister to a new identity and a new life. One in which Oakbourne would be nothing but memory, and the past would be nothing but ash.

The same pile of ash that was cooling in the grate right now.

She checked the little heart-shaped watch pinned to her bodice. The landlord would be here any moment, to take back the keys to the rooms she'd kept secret for four years. Rooms that had allowed her to conduct a very different side to the photographic trade she ran from her official studio, and in doing so gave her the most precious of commodities for a woman — independence.

That pile of white ash was her last connection to that sideline, and the postcards had been the first to hit the flames. Known as Frenchies in the trade, they were a fifty-fifty split of young women either challenging the viewer — blatantly inviting him to watch while they teased off their clothes and/or touched themselves — or the exact opposite — a range of what-the-butler-saws projecting purity personified, where the girls appeared to have no idea they were being watched. Whether reaching for a towel as they stepped out of a bath or innocently undressing for bed, they allowed the viewer to imagine himself peering through a half-open door or a crack in the curtain. He catches a glimpse of smooth thighs, round buttocks, pert breasts, all tantalisingly exposed. Anything beyond that, though, the pearls and oysters, so to speak, were merely hinted at in the postcards, ensuring the collector keeps on collecting.

Next in the fire went the names of Julia's models. As far as the purchasing public was concerned, here we have The Swedish Princess taking a bath, Scheherazade preparing herself for her lover, or The Rose of Shanghai going about her daily routine. If their real names got out, though, and one of the collectors tracked their address, who knows what might follow? Every link to the past must be destroyed, including a veritable fortune in the flip books she'd compiled. This was a new development within the industry. A series of thirty photographs, each slightly different from the next, bound together in such a way that, when the pages were flipped through at speed, the girl appeared to be moving.

*Come on, come on! Weren't landlords supposed to be prompt?*

She smoothed the runner on the table, then the antimacassars over the backs of the chairs, followed by the doilies and all the other fiddly crochet fripperies that she hated. Photographers by their nature need to be thorough, but when that photographer is a woman competing in a man's world, they need to be double, triple, twenty times thorough. Over the course of the past four years, meticulousness had become second nature to Julia, so for the umpteenth time she checked everything from the welsh dresser to the bookcase to the carved writing bureau where she'd kept records of her illicit income, away from the prying eyes of the police. Now that fingerprinting was starting to clinch cases, it was vital every item in these rented rooms was left gleaming and —

A shot rang out.

Julia jumped.

Of course it wasn't a gun! She really must stop flinching every time a door slammed, or a cab driver cracked his whip, or, in this case, a sash window came slamming down. A month had passed now. Four weeks in which funerals had been held, flowers had been laid, prayers had been said, tears had been shed. More tears than one person should cry in a lifetime. But grief is the price you pay for caring, and since there's no changing the past, it was time to take control of the future.

A trunk, of course, attracts too much attention. A leather satchel, though, paired with a blue and gold carpet bag swung with nonchalance, smacks of a casual overnight stay. Let Her Majesty's finest take the bones out of that, because in the end, everything that mattered fitted in both bags. Clothes she could buy. New camera, equipment. Hats, of course. Shoes. Costly though the replacements might be, the only necessities were money, passport and a few basic grooming items, along with Sam Whitmore's photograph in its silver frame. It wasn't, after all, as if she was unprepared. Escape had always been in the planning.

So why was it so hard to breathe?

Blaming the late summer heatwave (not to mention her new rib-crushing corset), Julia latched the delinquent window, noting how the late summer sun highlighted the indentations her tripod had left in the carpet. Happily, padded footstools were expressly designed for covering such marks, but in case the landlord's beady eye picked up on them — unlikely in a room wallpapered in oppressive green flock, but you never know — she'd plonked a plant pot on top to draw the focus. An aspidistra, dying from either too much water or too little, who knows? Lily had been the one who nursed the vile thing, a task that clearly Julia wasn't up to. In quiet moments, between

9

the cries of the rag-and-bone man, the shouts of the delivery drivers and the rumble of the goods trains passing by, she swore she could hear it pleading to be put out of its misery.

Out of nowhere, Lily's voice echoed in her memory.

*Bloke ran up to me the other night. Said, "Have you seen a policeman?" I told him, "Sorry, mate, I haven't seen anyone." He said, "Good. Stick 'em up!"*

It shouldn't hurt like this. There shouldn't still be knives ripping through Julia's stomach, simply because Lily would never pose for her again. There shouldn't be claws tearing out her innards because Nellie, Daisy, Birdie or indeed any of her models weren't coming back. But there were.

It hurt like buggery.

And Lily's bones might lie cold in her coffin, but what grave could quash the spirit of a girl who cracked non-stop jokes while she teased down a stocking or tweaked her nipple, breasts wobbling like two enormous white blancmanges with every pose she struck for the camera?

*'I was up before the judge last week for picking pockets. He fined me £5, so I told him, "Sorry m'lud, I've only got two quid on me. But if you could give me ten minutes with the crowd..."'*

*Lily, Lily, Lily. I'll bet you've got the worms in stitches.*

Sniffing back the tears, Julia forced herself to concentrate on the practicalities in hand. Any chemicals she hadn't been able to flush down the lavatory, she'd lugged back to her studio, before dismantling the makeshift dark room and generally making sure the landlord would never suspect his Turkish rug had seen more frilly bloomers than a French lingerie shop. Or his big, deep, comfy sofa had welcomed more than its fair share of girls draped in saucy positions. Much less that his brass bed had accommodated numerous pretty young creatures, who the camera would have you believe were frolicking alone.

If flip books were taking the world of peep shows by storm, it was nothing compared to the prospect of moving pictures. Between Edison Studios on the other side of the Atlantic and the Lumière Brothers on this, the advances of celluloid film was making rip-roaring progress, and if Julia had been able to stick around long enough to sell her pile of flip books, she might have earned enough to buy a stake in the business. Still, it was not to be. In the fire they went, ashes to ashes, dust to dust, and all that.

She smoothed her skirts, brown cotton trimmed with copper, just enough pattern on the fabric to be chic, just the right cut to be elegant, just enough elegance not to be noticed. In five hours and seven minutes, the hands of her watch told her, she'd be on the train bound for London, satisfied in the knowledge that no one would notice her absence for two, three, possibly four days. Because from fire, doth the phoenix arise. Or put it another way: from others' misfortune, doth one's own luck perk up.

Take the night before last. A window had been left open in one of the houses round the corner. A candle left burning. A curtain blowing beside it. Come midnight, the whole house was ablaze, neighbours forming human chains in their nightshirts, pumping the horse troughs like crazy. Despite an army of firemen cracking out two hundred gallons a minute from each steam engine, the flames refused to go quietly. The occupants of the tiny end-terraced house, two old ladies skinny as sticks, had the presence of mind to shout for assistance, rather than try to salvage the possessions inside.

Living close by, Julia had no choice but to be acquainted with the two sisters, but honestly, they were the two most irritating women on the planet. Whenever she could, she'd duck into a shop, a workshop, a public house to avoid them. One notable time, she dived into a hedge.

Which is not to say there weren't opportunities to be grabbed.

'I have rooms to spare,' Julia had said. This was on the run up to dawn, when even the fire horses were tiring in the harness. 'You're welcome to stay with me until your place is habitable.'

'It'd only be a week, dear.'

'Yes, yes, no more than a week.'

In a week, Julia McAllister would no longer exist.

Lust was a generous employer, there was no doubt about that, and one to whom Julia was loathe to give notice. But the police were this close to discovering her past, despite how tight she was with a certain detective inspector after singlehandedly crushing a prostitution and drugs ring, as well putting a gang of thugs behind bars.

*If you kill a man and it's premeditated murder, you hang.*

Julia gave a final rub to the brass lampstand and the candlesticks on the mantelpiece, before giving the swagged drapes hanging from the oak pelmet rail a quick shake. Finally, she gave the ormulu clock on the mantelpiece one last turn of the key. Because while death and betrayal come from the closest of quarters, life, like it or not, does go on.

Outside, Julia switched the carpet bag to her right hand and the satchel to her left, and recalled that this time yesterday, the pall of smoke from the housefire was still giving the factories on the far side of Oakbourne a run for their money. The inevitable consequence of tons of wooden furniture cluttering the rooms, and by all accounts the old dears had plenty of clutter. But today, with the sun shining and not a cloud in the sky, only a blackened frontage and boarded windows testified to the disaster. And instead of fire bells, cries and the clatter of buckets, the Common resounded with the joyful yelps of small boys spinning tops, nannies cooing over their charges as they pushed perambulators, and dogs yapping with delight as they rolled round in the mud resulting from the firemen's hoses.

Watching a pair of squirrels chase each other round, then up, an oak tree, while the ducks on the pond quacked and spiky green conkers split open on the horse chestnuts to reveal their glossy treasures, Julia wondered, would she have made the offer, had she been staying? Would she hell. But allowing Mitzi and Minzi, Bitsy and Betsy, Izzy and Busy, whatever their names were, unrestricted access to the premises gave her more breathing space than she could possibly have hoped for.

Approaching her shop (or more accurately, what used to be her shop, it was a past life now, remember?) she crossed her lacy gloved fingers that the old ducks would be out, directing operations while workers cleared the debris from their house.

'Oh, you're back!'

'She's back.'

'We dusted the shop from top to bottom while you were gone.' The taller of the two (Mitzi? Bitsy?) wagged a black ostrich feather duster. 'Even the china dogs in the window.'

'Especially the china dogs in the window.'

Of course, when Julia said taller, the old bird still only came up to her shoulder. In fact, with their faded blue eyes, identical outfits and matching grey buns, that inch difference in height was pretty much the only thing that told them apart. She stashed her travel bags in the dark room and locked the door.

'Thank you.'

'Oh, please. No need to thank us.'

'No need.'

'We're very grateful to you for taking us in — this is most kind of you, dear.'

'Most kind.'

No smile could be tighter, or more of an effort to squeeze out. After just a few hours, this pair had ground Julia's nerves to powder faster than pepper in a mill, following her around like puppies, peering at her over glasses perched on the ends of their noses, with Minzi (Betsy?) repeating everything her sister said like Echo on bloody Olympus. Idly, she wondered if they'd escaped from the new asylum for the criminally insane, and had just been hiding out in that house down the road. Congenital arsonists, perhaps?

If so, that left a spare room in the asylum. Julia wondered if they would admit her without notice.

Oh, thank God. She spun round at the *ting!* of the bell over the door. Any diversion — ANY — to give her a break from these two. She couldn't stomach another four hours of this. But she was wrong — smiles, it turned out, could be tighter than hers, and more of an effort to squeeze out. You could practically hear this one pop.

'Detective Inspector Collingwood, what a lovely surprise.'

Shock was more accurate, and it was a long way from lovely. Even so, with cases needing to be closed on murderers, thugs, and prostitution rackets, all involving more meetings, paperwork and reports than the Boot Street Station had seen in its entire history, not to mention a never-ending round of court appearances, it was unlikely Collingwood had had time to sneeze, much less dig into Julia's background. The fingers in her gloved hand crossed tighter.

14

'Ladies.'

When he tipped his hat, the old dears all but swooned. Could you blame them? Confidence to the point of cocky can be very appealing. Add on a runner's frame and grey eyes that matched the colour of his suit, throw in a touch of pepper and salt at the temples and a strong chin that was, somewhat unusually for this day and age, clean shaven, and mix the whole shebang with authority, and you have magnetism on legs.

'Apologies for ending your appointment abruptly, but the shop is going to have to close —'

'Oh, we're not customers, Inspector.' Mitzi (Bitsy?) let out a girlish giggle. 'Mrs. McAllister is our landlady.'

'Very nice landlady, too,' Minzi (Betsy?) added.

Goldfish was the image that sprang to mind, the way Collingwood's mouth opened and closed.

'Of course you are.' His expressionless grey eyes fixed on Julia. 'Can't imagine why I thought otherwise. You still need to shut up shop.'

With unexpected tact, the old girls grabbed each other's arms and fluttered off into the kitchen, closing the door behind them.

'Let's make it four o'clock, shall we?' Julia felt for the train ticket in her purse. 'Only I have an urgent appointment —'

'I need you, Julia, and I need you now.'

'My goodness, John, you could at least buy me dinner first!'

For a second there, she thought he was going to smile. For another second, she thought he would lean in and kiss her.

'They've found a body. A woman. Behind the old theatre. I need you to take photographic records, before more evidence gets trampled and destroyed.'

Above the smell of the freesias in the vase, Julia picked up the resiny scent of his cologne, William Pengalion's *Hammam Bouquet*, unless she missed her guess. Blended to invoke images of sultans and harems, sultry steam baths, and boudoirs reeking of sex.

'I'm really sorry, but this appointment —'

'I'm not asking, Julia. Fetch your camera.'

# Chapter 2

In its heyday, the Apollo Theatre showcased Shakespeare and Dickens to a packed house of six hundred, drawing many a famous actress and actor. Ugly red brick outside, the proscenium inside dazzled with gilded scrollwork and velvet. But once the railway established itself as a fixture in Oakbourne, serving factories and mills that were constantly expanding at the very time theatres ceased to be the preserve of the lower classes, the Apollo was abandoned in favour of a grand new development, all pillars and arches and wide sweeping steps, complete with dining halls, a ballroom, a restaurant (naturally), and the finest galleried concert hall outside Central London. Other changes followed the throb of the rail. Musical comedy rode roughshod over the classics, music halls elbowed tradition aside, and burlesque trampled convention to dust. These days, only the rats were treading what few boards remained in the derelict building.

For the past thirty minutes, Julia had blocked out the gagging stench of congealed blood, the stink of rotting vegetation, the flies, the unnatural twisting of the woman's limbs, the ravaging of small animals — just as she'd blocked out the reminder of other recent deaths. People close to her. People that she'd cared for. Most of all Julia blocked out the fact that, until yesterday, this had been a living, breathing human being with the same hopes and fears and dreams that drove us all, and had concentrated purely on photographic technique.

*Insert the glass plate. Slide the cover from its holder. Expose the lens, a fraction of a second is all that is needed, then replace the cover and remove. Another plate ready for processing.*

It was a mantra she repeated over and over in her head, as she captured the scene from every angle with detached, but rapid efficiency. From the moment Collingwood first mooted the idea of Boot Street employing a crime scene photographer, the professional in Julia couldn't resist planning how she'd tackle the task. True, she didn't have access to one of those specialised tripods that allowed the Parisian police to photograph corpses from above, but that was hardly surprising, given that the French were still pioneering the system.

'Has she been moved?' Julia asked.

Standing on the sidelines, his grey tailored worsted standing out like royalty down a coal mine among the knee-high thistles and rubble, Collingwood shook his head.

'The tramp who found the body realised straight away that she was dead.' With the back of her head caved in and the skin mottled and black, it didn't take a doctor to work that one out. 'He lost no time reporting his gruesome discovery to Boot Street, and once my sergeant confirmed his story, I gave my men strict instructions to stay clear until you were finished.'

All Julia could think of was, thank God it wasn't a child who had found her. Waste spaces like this make for fantastic playgrounds, as do abandoned theatres. Especially abandoned theatres whose windows served as target practice for stones, and whose crumbling masonry made terrific castles and forts.

Julia slotted another plate in the camera. Distancing yourself from murder isn't difficult when your mind's on a train ticket, your emotions are hidden under a heavy cloth, and everything you're recording is upside down. In fact, it was almost easy to pretend there was nothing to bracket this with different violent deaths and different pools of blood...

Sooner or later, though, the old truism kicks in. *You can run, but you can't hide.*

You can't hide from the reality that this woman had been dumped behind the theatre like the rubbish. That as a consequence, she'd been stripped of every shred of dignity, exposed to being prodded and poked by all manner of people, photographed, talked about, gawped over, debated. And — given the location, along with her cheap corset and patched drawers — quite likely forgotten before the week was out, buried without a name on her headstone or a family to mourn her, and her attacker, even worse, never found.

'That means,' Julia said, 'the killer moved the body after she was dead.'

Upside down on the image, she watched Collingwood stiffen.

'What makes you say that?'

It wouldn't be for lack of trying on Collingwood's part if the killer got away. Ambitious detectives never give up, and doggedness ran through to his marrow — which was at least some small comfort to Julia's conscience. Knowing that, when she boarded that train in a few hours' time, it wouldn't be her fault that this murder would join a long line where the odds of being solved were hundreds to one. No witnesses, no evidence, no means of identifying the victim, since she had few clothes, no reticule, not so much as a cross round her neck.

Julia would have played her part, taking crime scene photographs. The rest was down to the police.

Having said that, the victim still deserved Collingwood's best shot at justice, and considering he'd have to waste precious time finding another photographer to develop the negatives, passing on the points her keen eye had picked up on was the least she could do.

'You can come over now, I've finished photographing this quadrant.' *Quadrant. Did you hear that?* Julia asked the body at their feet. *That's how impersonal the bastard who did this has made you.* She turned her face to the sky. *Breathe, breathe. Don't let it get to you...* 'If your tramp found her here,' she said levelly, 'then the pool of blood over there says that's where she was attacked, and given the massive wounds on her head, if she'd staggered or crawled, blood would have poured everywhere.'

'And since dead bodies don't bleed, she was moved after death.'

'Moved a lot, unless I miss my guess.' Disentangling herself from a buddleia bush, so beloved of places that themselves were unloved, Julia pointed out how everywhere else, the weeds were high and had gone to seed, but between the victim and the blood pool, they'd been flattened in a ragged pattern.

'Could have been a struggle,' Collingwood said. 'She wouldn't be the first victim who fought for her life.'

'Had it purely been the grime and filth stuck to her undergarments, I might be tempted to agree.'

'But since you've never agreed with me from the day we met...'

'It's not easy being right, John, but someone's got to do it.' In spite of everything, Julia smiled. 'See the way her hair's matted with dirt? She's been rolled around so much, the dust has effectively become plaster of Paris, sealing the wound. And where's her dress?'

'What's your theory?'

'What makes you think I have one?'

'Am I wrong?'

Julia pressed the shutter release, changed the plate, took another, then another, then another. 'A dead body weighs the same as a live one,' she said, 'but when you try to move it, the centre of gravity shifts to whatever point you're supporting the load, making it almost impossible to move.'

She'd found that out from experience.

'The difference,' he murmured, 'between say, picking up a hundredweight block of wood and a hundredweight bag of ball bearings, where you're having to adjust your balance and grip ten times a second?'

'Exactly. And when that bag of ball bearings is limp, lolling and bumping all over the place, it's exhausting.'

*Believe me, oh believe me, it's exhausting.* It took her an hour, possibly longer, before she got enough breath back to start covering the Devil's grave with stones. But that was long ago...

She knelt beside the woman's body. 'That's when the killer got sloppy.'

In the branches of the trees that were intent on taking over the site, sparrows tutted, hopped and scolded. A couple of bravehearts took mudbaths, regardless of the intrusion of privacy.

'Sloppy, eh?' Collingwood hunkered down beside her.

'Look at this.'

'The fragment of mauve silk trapped under the body?'

'Exactly.'

'So?'

'So he killed her, pulled off her skirt — which is lavender, by the way, not mauve, it's all the rage this season — then he pulled off her petticoats, her shoes and her jacket, but like I said, dead weight's hard to manoeuvre. As he grew tired, he grew sloppy, and the fabric ripped. Although quite frankly, Inspector, I'm amazed you hadn't noticed those things.'

'Who said I hadn't.'

'Really? Then why the look of surprise? Because I took photographs lying horizontal with the victim to ensure no evidence escaped the scrutiny of my lens?' *And to see what the victim saw in her final moments.*

'No.'

'Because I'm caked in dust and filth from rolling on the ground?'

'Not that, either.'

'What then?'

A muscle twitched at the side of his mouth. 'I'm simply surprised that it took you so long, Mrs. McAllister, to realise you'd missed your vocation.'

# Chapter 3

Shuffling through the Walton Street Arcade, sun streaming through the arched glass roof, a man with a face far older than his years caught his reflection in the watchmaker's bow window. The hair under his battered Fedora was still curly, dark and plentiful, but the suit that used to be a perfect fit hung loose, worn almost through to holes, and the right lens in his spectacles was broken in a zigzag. Shaken and ashamed in equal measures, he shuffled on in shoes he'd taken from the dead man he'd found hanging underneath a bridge. Two sizes too big, but the suicide wouldn't be needing them. He couldn't remember the last time he'd worn socks.

Long long ago, he had been Aaron Adelman. That was when he had brothers and sisters, a mother and father, four loving grandparents, as well as aunts, uncles and cousins. Last month, though, he was Daniel Carpenter, last week Isaac Cook, and today he went by Ira Miller. There was no disguising his Jewish heritage — his eyes, his nose, his face told the story, so why hide it? The surnames he'd picked, though, were all trades of some kind. Mason, Baker, Cooper, Skinner. Common, anonymous, and, from his point of view, easy to remember, but none of the names he'd adopted were from his own trade.

He stopped at another bow window, this time a jewellery shop with a giant wooden eagle stretching its wings over the doorway. He leaned closer. The pieces in the window weren't a patch on his work. Pretty enough, he supposed. Shell drop earrings, pearl necklaces, lockets that remained perennially popular with the ladies, and finely engraved they were, too, he might add. Especially the one third from left, showing a heron stalking among the reeds.

He moved on, before someone came out and moved him on. To be honest, he wouldn't blame them.

He enjoyed coming here. The grandeur and glass reminded him of happier days, when he'd stroll the Burlington Arcade in central London, past fancy establishments selling hosiery, shoes, gloves and hats, swinging his cane without a care in the world. Days when he had a family and a permanent roof over his head. Days when he turned diamonds and sapphires, rubies and emeralds into exquisite pieces of jewellery. And the days before that, as well, when he was growing up above his father's shirtmaker's shop in Jermyn Street, and often, when he closed his eyes at night, could still smell the woody scent of tobacco from the customers' cigars.

Now look at him! Reduced to doss houses sleeping ten, sometimes twelve, to a room, and invariably taking shifts for the bed. Sadly, slums like that were all he could afford, and to take his mind off the farts and the snoring, the bed bugs and mould, he'd remember Poppa, beavering away in the back room in shirt sleeves and cravat, ready to drop the iron, whisk off his flat cap and pull on a smart tailored jacket, if a gentleman came through the door. How many times had he wondered if the same old stove was still coughing away in the corner? Whether the rack beside the counter still showcased thirty collar styles? If Poppa and Mama were still alive...

Slopping along in his too-big shoes, past establishments similar to Burlington, but selling confectionary, tea, corsets and fine china, he was conscious of the contemptuous glances thrown his way. Of neatly barbered men in expensive tailored lounge suits, looking down their noses at his shaggy beard and faded tie. Ladies in their frills and flounces and leg o'mutton sleeves, lips curling at the meat pie clutched tightly in his left hand for his lunch. Eight years ago, he'd have done the same, no doubt —

'No, no, no.' His startled fingers let go of the pie, splattering gravy over the flagstones and the dead man's shoes. 'It can't be.'

A jeweller's eye has to be keen, but that's for work that is close-up and magnified many times over. Distance is a different matter, but even so. The head on one side? The swing of the hips? He broke into a run to catch up with the woman in the lavender dress, but at the entrance to the arcade, a greengrocer's boy came out of nowhere. Vegetable marrows went flying. Curses flew, too. By the time he had skirted the barrow, the woman was swallowed up by the crowd. Not before he saw her face, though.

'How?' he asked himself, slumping down on the ground. 'How is it possible? How can she be alive, when I heard her last breath leave her body?'

# Chapter 4

When Julia got back to the shop, she was greeted by a tantalising array of savoury smells. Needless to say, it wasn't the only thing that met her.

'Nice Welsh rarebit for your lunch, dear — oh my goodness!'

'You poor dear darling girl, what happened?'

'Were you run over?'

'Are you hurt?'

'I'm not sure those stains will come out.'

'Even with blue bags and bleach.'

'That tear on your skirt will need professional mending.'

Julia gritted her teeth and forced a smile. 'This?' No matter how many times she shook her skirts, clouds of dust still rose high enough to make St. Peter cough. 'This, ladies, is a warning not to go rolling on patches of waste ground with a corpse.'

The old ladies burst into giggles. 'We must remember not to do that in the future.'

'Yes, we must!'

'You run along and tidy yourself up, dear. We'll have the rarebit on the table when you're finished.' Mitzi (Bitsy?) glanced coyly at the constable charged with helping lug Julia's equipment back to the shop — Collingwood stayed at the Apollo to supervise the collection of evidence and removal of the body. 'Shall we rustle up enough for two?'

'Easily done,' gushed her sister. 'We have a refreshing orange custard for dessert.'

Leaving the constable reluctantly declining the offer of a meal that apparently knocked spots off the stale ham and tongue sandwich his wife had made, Julia locked the plates in the dark room and glanced at the clock. She still had stacks of time — and how long had it been since she'd had a Welsh rarebit?

'Smells delicious,' she said truthfully. 'Hope there's enough there for seconds.'

Up in her room though, her mood swiftly changed. If you didn't know better, you'd say nothing was different. When people — by which she meant the police — by which she meant Collingwood — looked around, they'd see day dresses, jackets and blouses hanging in the wardrobe. Chemises, stockings and corsets layered neatly in the chest, interspersed with sprigs of lavender to keep them smelling fresh. They'd see hats in boxes, shoes on racks, paper, ink and blotter on the writing desk. Everything pointing to a woman who'd slipped out to buy a feather boa or a bar of soap and would be home within the hour. It was the same with the shop, with the dark room, the properties room, and the studio, which used to be the morning room, where she took portraits of couples, families, children and dogs (Pomeranians, mostly). Spick and span wasn't the word.

A little too tidy, Collingwood might think. But think was all he could do. Unless...

He had a sharp eye and an even sharper memory. When her models were being picked off one by one and Julia was his prime suspect, he'd searched this house top to bottom a hundred times over. Would he remember the photograph on the mantelpiece in her room? The man in the silver frame who Julia pretended was still alive, so she could continue to run Whitmore Photographic? If he noticed its absence, he'd know she was in the wind.

By then, though, she'd be in Paris. Or Vienna. Or a boat bound for New York.

In her new life, there would be no stiff, formal portraits paying the rent. No selling china dogs to put food on the table. She would travel so far and so wide, her feet wouldn't touch the ground as she compiled the book that was her dream. Not simply photographs showcasing ancient cities and lost civilizations, alongside mysterious tribes and cultures. Julia wanted to push out the boundaries. Have people compare the plight of poverty-stricken Welsh miners against, say, the greed-driven miners of Tombstone. Show them the contrasts in such a way they could actually feel them, and then, just when they thought they'd seen the whole picture, turn perception on its head by showing the hardships and horror of the Alaskan Gold Rush, for example, where three thousand pack animals died in one valley alone, to the point where it was called Dead Horse Gulch.

Ditching her filthy clothes, a ripple ran down Julia's backbone. It wasn't fear that she mightn't make a clean getaway — you don't spend four years in the mucky picture trade without making contacts in the forgery business as well. The passport in her carpet bag was for one Jennifer James (Mrs.). Something else made her spine tingle as she scrubbed the grime from her skin. For one silly minute, she thought it might be regret.

'Moind if I walk with yer, then?'

Julia did mind. She minded a lot. She'd barely put down her fork after lunch — the old dears were right, by the way, that orange custard was refreshing — when an earnest young thing with a mass of the blackest curls you've ever seen struggling to stay inside the ribbon at her nape, came barrelling into the shop. Her name was Miss Keane, she said breathlessly, she was a reporter, and is it true Whitmore Photographic was under contract to take scene of crime photos? If she could have an interview with Sam Whitmore, it would make her career.

Picturing Sam's grave in neighbouring Southolt, Julia was inclined to agree.

'Tomorrow,' she promised. 'Ten o'clock sharp.'

'Heavens to Blarney, termorrer's no good.' Miss Keane rolled her earnest black eyes. 'No other police force in the country has entertained such a notion, not even the Met. I need to be quick off the mark for me scoop.'

'Ten o'clock, take it or leave it.'

The little sharp chin that seemed permanently pointed upwards tipped another two inches. 'Yer give me no choice, I'll be round on the dot, but yerself now. Mrs. McAllister, am I right?'

Julia nodded.

'Scottish meets Oirish. Who'd have thought such a thing! Anyway, you'll give me an interview, won't yer? About the French women, I mean.'

That was an easy hook to wriggle off. 'I don't know any French women.'

'Is that so?' The woman scrabbled back through her notes. 'Well, darn and darnation, I couldda sworn someone told me you'd taken the French sisters in after the fire.'

*Ah.* Passing it off as a joke, Julia assured her intense little visitor that she'd be delighted to give her an interview. In fact, the instant Miss Keane had finished with Mr. Whitmore, Julia would —

'Today, today. I gotta put a piece in today!'

'Not possible, I'm afraid. I have an appointment in town.'

Which was when Little Miss Glue said, 'Moind if I walk with yer, then?'

Now, had Julia been going to collect photographic supplies or take a breath of fresh air, then yes, the aptly named Miss Keane would have been welcome to tag along. A stroll round the Common, feed the pigeons, take a cup of tea together, admire the latest fashions, who knows? But not when there's a train to be caught, and awkward questions to be asked about satchels and carpet bags.

Julia made a decision. 'Fifteen minutes,' she said. 'That's all I can spare —'

'Ach, that's wonderful. Wonderful. Yer have no idea what a boggin hard slog it is, trying to make yer way in a man's world. I tell yer, making a good fist of a job's not enough. Yer have to prove yerself twenty times over, and for a fraction of what they pay the men.'

'Which paper do you work for?'

'Me? No, no, no. Yer'll not catching me being tied to one place! Roving reporter, that's Orla Keane, because interesting stories cover any manner of distance, and crime don't have a conscience about straying past police boundaries, that it does not.'

*Freelance? Well, well.* 'Good for you.'

'Why, thank you, Mrs. McAllister!' Miss Keane was so pleased with the compliment, that the ribbon at her neck sprung loose, spilling more hair than one hat should be forced to put up with. ''Cause the way I see it is this. Man or woman, we've all got to do our own growing, no matter how tall yer ole grandpappy was.'

'Sounds like yours was a giant.'

'Wonderful man, absolutely wonderful. Just wish me six brothers back home was like him, but Mary, Mother of Jaysus, they're always fightin' one other, that lot. Always, always, always.'

'None of them get on?'

'Sure they do. They just can't find no one else to fight with.'

'Gosh, time's up.' Julia resisted the urge to slap herself on the back for ducking the interview. 'See you in the morning, then, ten o'clock sharp.'

'On the button.' Miss Keane had a lovely smile when she put her mind to it. 'Oh, hey! I nearly forgot. Yer never got to telling me about the French women.'

Julia glanced at the clock. Five minutes, no more, and even then she'd have to run to the station. It was better than having this little leech sticking to her, though. Quickly and succinctly, Julia ran through the events, followed by her offer of a roof over the sisters' heads until they were straight, and what a pleasure, an absolute delight, it was to have them stay with her, she only wished it was longer.

'Ach, that's brilliant. I'm grateful for this. You're a star.'

Miss Keane held out her hand. Julia shook it.

'You, too, Miss Keane.'

'Orla,' she said. 'Now we're friends, you have to call me Orla, only for the love of Blarney, please don't say it.'

'Say what?'

'Orla nothing.'

Julia was still laughing when she arrived at the station, satchel over her shoulder, ticket between her teeth, carpet bag in hand.

Just in time to watch the train pull away from the platform.

# Chapter 5

Don't let anyone tell you otherwise, glass negatives are heavy. Which is why Julia needed Collingwood's help to cart them over to the Apollo, and why a constable helped carry them back.

And don't let them tell you developing isn't a messy, smelly business, either. When you're used to the stench of acids and chemicals, though, you tend not to notice, and in the warm red light of the darkroom, flanked by shelves groaning with bromide and potassium and soda carbonate crystals, surrounded by with mortars and pestles, jugs, scales and hoses, Julia set to work.

Thanks to one of those brand new horseless carriages losing control by the railway bridge and crashing on to the tracks, no trains would be running until the following morning. In the interim, she was damned if she was just going to sit back and do nothing, when she could be closing the gap between justice and victim, even if it was by just the tiniest margin.

So she moistened the plates, dunked them in the developing fluid, agitating them gently from time to time until the image appeared on the glass, and transferring the negatives to a bath of fixing solution. *Voila!* Now it was only a question of slipping the paper under the negative in a special developing frame, taking them to her studio and waiting for daylight to work its magic. Once the picture appeared, the print would be washed, treated so the silver from the plate was converted into a more stable compound, washed again, fixed again, then hung on a line to dry.

It was a production line that was absorbing, time-consuming, challenging and enjoyable. Julia knew she'd be working right through the night.

'Steak and kidney pudding for dinner,' Minzi/Betsy/Izzy informed her, when Julia took a break to come up for air, which in itself was a mistake — the sisters absolutely reeked of gardenia. 'Or beef and onion pie, if you prefer.'

'Suet crust,' her sister said.

'With gravy.'

'And crisp roast potatoes.'

'No, really, you shouldn't have.' Julia said, and she meant it. Irritating though they were, the sisters' house had burned through, yet here they were, acting like they hadn't a care in the world.

'We didn't, dear. It was the neighbours.'

'They read about your generosity in the newspaper, and since none of them wanted to be outdone —'

'— they're plying us with food.'

'There's an Irish stew as well.'

'Only it looked a bit greasy.'

'And a fish pie from Number 28.' The younger one sniffed. 'Straight in the dustbin, that. Never washes her hands, her.'

'Well meaning, mind.'

'Very well meaning,' her sister agreed. 'But the fish pie stays in the bin.'

The neighbours had obviously had a whip round for clothes, too. The old dears were neatly decked out in matching blue cotton blouses, with darker blue piping running in vertical stripes, and little navy blue bows at the neck.

'Her from 34 gave us some scent.'

'I'd noticed.'

'Gardenia it is —'

'— oh and sherry.' The older sister tipped her head on one side, as though asking a question.

Sherry wasn't halfway strong enough to counteract the horrible pong of Gardenia, much less the ache in Julia's heart.

'Personally, I'm more inclined towards something harder.'

'Lucky her at Number 45 brought that along, then!'

Exchanging giggles that suggested the sisters had been worried Julia's home was a temperance establishment, they whisked a bottle of single malt out of the cupboard and poured three generous glasses. Very smooth it was too, and it was undoubtedly down to Messrs. Bowmore (from Islay) that both the pudding and the pie were attacked without mercy, no quarter given to either.

'Come with me,' Julia said, when they'd finished.

'Ooh, I'm not sure I can.'

It wasn't clear whether Mitzy/Bitzy was referring to her bloated stomach or the copious amounts of undiluted whisky she'd knocked back, but with the sisters hanging on to Julia like sheets in a gale, she steered her giggling lodgers in to the studio. There wasn't time to change the backdrop, not with the workload ahead, so instead of pretty painted balustrades and urns bursting with flowers, they were stuck with an artist's impression of the newly commissioned HMS *Prince George*. It was astonishingly popular with retired sea captains, whether naval, commercial or imaginary, and it seemed fitting that the old girls just happened to be three sheets to the wind in front of a battleship.

'You're taking our picture!'

'No one's ever taken our picture!'

'After the lovely things you said about us in the newspaper, too.'

*Tweet, tweet, tweet, like a pair of bloody sparrows.*

'We cut out the article.'

'We're going to frame it.'

'Ever so nice it'll look, on the mantelpiece in the living room.'

'Next to this portrait.'

'Pride of place!'

Julia rigged up her tripod, thinking, *What was it Oscar Wilde said? No good deed goes unpunished?* Being poked with pitchforks in hell for eternity was preferable to just one more day under the same roof as these two. *Tell me, does Satan sell tickets?*

'Should we smile?'

'No, no, we don't smile, dear. We'll go on, then, just a little one.'

'Should we hold hands?'

'Let's link arms.'

Blocking out the incessant twittering, Julia concentrated on lighting, angles and pose, amazed that such a simple act could bring so much pleasure in old age. Oh, the relief! the silence! though, after they'd tottered off. It crossed Julia's mind that their house had committed suicide, unable to take any more, but strangely the sisters' presence around the place kept Julia's heartbreak at bay and stopped the ghosts here from walking. As did her work on the crime scene, and for the first time, she stopped to study the prints pegged out on the line, seeing them as photographs in their own right, rather than links in a chain of production.

Not all the plates had been developed, but as Julia examined them, a picture slowly emerged of what had transpired between killer and victim.

*I'm simply surprised that it took you so long, Mrs. McAllister, to realise you'd missed your vocation.*

Perhaps Collingwood was right, because Julia was proud of the way these shots contributed towards a cast iron case. Out of professional curiosity, she'd researched the way the Parisian police pioneered this new technology, and was excited by the chance to copy their methods. Was it because she saw life through an artist's eye, encapsulating emotions rather than just people, even when taking a portrait, that made her instinctively add touches of her own? From the outset, she was determined that every angle of the crime scene would be chronicled for posterity. Every detail captured without contamination of evidence, thereby eliminating recourse to police notes that weren't always complete, and reliance on memories that themselves became unreliable over time.

Tragic though the circumstances were, these photographs had become witnesses after the fact. God willing, they would bring the dead woman vengeance.

Most of Aaron's friendships had drifted apart, once he took to the road. His friends had married, had children, settled into routines in which there was no room for someone dipping in and out of their schedules. Life grew lonelier with every trip.

Until Gigi.

From the moment he saw her, kicking up her legs in a chorus line, he knew she was The One. The woman for whom he'd give everything up.

He could still see her, lying at his feet. Heard the last breath wheeze from her throat. But he should have made sure. Because the dead don't walk, and they don't swing their hips.

# Chapter 6

'Oh God, no!' Julia clamped both hands over her mouth. 'Not another body.'

'Murder? No.' Collingwood tossed his hat on the rack by the door. 'What made you think that?'

Lily, Nellie, Birdie — the girls she'd photographed, butchered in quick succession over the past few months, that's what made her think that. 'It's not often the long arm of the law taps on my window at midnight.' Julia's heart might be pounding twenty-five to the dozen, but her voice was level and calm.

'Midnight?' Collingwood seemed genuinely shocked. 'My apologies. I was passing, saw a light — I'll leave.'

'Nonsense. I'm developing the negatives from the crime scene, and will be for quite a while yet.' She toyed with the idea of putting the kettle on. Instead, she dug out the forty-year old cognac she kept under the counter. 'How's your daughter?'

The cockiness drained from a face that turned as grey as Collingwood's eyes. 'Every week the doctor says it will be her last. Every week my little fighter refuses to listen.'

'But?'

He rubbed his forehead and pinched the bridge of his nose. 'Tuberculosis is a bugger, it really is. Eleven years old, and the poor kid's nothing but a bag of bones, with skin so thin you can see her veins. A living skeleton.' He sank the cognac in one hit. 'Listening to her hacking ... watching her vomit up nothing...' He poured himself another glass. 'Emily, my wife, is deeply religious. Too deeply in my opinion, but that's another matter. The point is, when she isn't trying to coax Alice to drink lemonade or take soup, or wiping her clean or changing the sheets —'

'She still won't entertain the idea of a nurse?'

'Ah, well. Be gentle, as a nursing mother tenderly cares for her own children. Saint Paul's letter to the Thessalonians, she reliably informs me. Chapter two, verse seven, if you must know, and then, of course, there's Proverbs. Her children arise and call her blessed. That's thirty-one, by the way.'

Out of nowhere, different scriptures flew at Julia, attacking like malevolent bats.

*The sun shall be turned into darkness and the moon into blood.*

There were others. Many others. Every last one in the name of the Lord.

Julia pushed the scriptures away, as she'd pushed away the man who used to quote them. Quote them at the end of his fist, until one day she could no longer stand by and watch her mother and brother beaten to paste, while waiting for the bastard to rape her. Fourteen or not, she set a trap for her stepfather, shot him dead, then buried him in an unmarked grave.

Sooner or later, Collingwood would find out, and Julia was damned if she'd hang for that monster. But tonight Collingwood was too busy fighting demons of his own, and her heart went out to him.

'According to my wife, these ulcerated lungs are my fault. She's convinced that the sins I investigate stick to me, and that's the cause of Alice's consumption. Since she won't listen to reason, and I won't resign from the police force, she now spends every waking moment praying for God to make Alice better.'

'You don't believe, though?'

'In a god who tortures children? Hell, no.'

Once more, Julia sensed a but. She waited.

'But if I did, I'd ask Him to take her. Take her tonight, now, to show the same compassion He apparently wants us to have, only, please, in the name of pity, put an end to my little girl's torment. I'd ask Him — Christ, I'd beg Him on my knees — to take my life in exchange for hers.' Collingwood's tortured eyes met Julia's. 'Except it doesn't work that way, does it? There's no going back with that wretched White Plague, and no deals to be made with God or the Devil.'

Julia wasn't so sure about that. She'd had her own run-in with the Devil. She'd promised her mother and brother he'd never hurt anyone again, emptied the chamber of a British Bulldog revolver into his heart to prove it, then piled rocks on the grave to make sure. As deals go, she was content with the bargain, and had she not been committed to finishing the plates in the dark room, she would have led Collingwood upstairs. A good bounce round the bed sheets would give them both much-needed release, and be as fine a way as any for Mrs. McAllister to tie off her the ends of her life here in Oakbourne, before making the transition to Mrs. James.

She knew there'd be no guilt on his part.

'How's the investigation going?' she asked instead.

'Progress is slow, and that's an understatement.' He swirled the Courvoisier around in the glass, watching the light from the lamp play on the colours. Amber, gold, yellow and russet, evoking images of sunsets on a woodland floor in late autumn. 'Considering where she was found, we think she was probably a prostitute, which means that in all likelihood she was killed on Saturday night.'

Julia nodded. That was the busiest time for working girls, and it made sense for the woman to choose a nice, quiet location to carry out her business, because they can't all afford hotels by the hour, or have rooms to take their clients.

'The trouble is, my men have asked around, but no one fitting the description appears to be missing, which is not in itself unusual. Working girls often disappear for days on end, but that's why I knocked tonight. Perhaps if we showed the pimps and the street-walkers a photo...?'

Julia thought of the battered face that had been dragged over weeds and stones and twelve years of waste. Cloudy eyes. Skin black where the blood in her body had pooled. 'Better to have a portrait taken in the mortuary, after she's been cleaned up a bit.'

'Not necessarily.' Collingwood perched on the edge of the counter and swung one leg back and forth. 'For one thing, having examined her hands, her teeth, her hair and her skin, and not finding any signs of — how can I put this? — the victim being a lady in the gentlefolk sense, I'm pretty sure the crowds she hung out with have seen worse. Much worse, to be honest.'

Julia pictured the fight for survival that took place on a daily basis — hourly sometimes — on the other side of the canal. It was a different world over there. A world of factories and mills, belching smoke from the chimneys. A world of dangerous dark alleyways, teeming with brothels and opium dens, and crawling with drunks, pickpockets and all manner of predators. A world in which families were thrown out of their homes as a consequence of industrial accidents that were not their fault, reduced to begging and thieving under the arches.

'And for another, time's not on my side,' Collingwood was saying. 'Suppose the killer's working the barges? By the time any spruced-up photos are ready to be touted round, he could be halfway to Northampton.'

'Oakbourne is a town with two faces, remember. On one side are the barges and dark alleys, but on this side we have a pretty Saxon church, with its equally pretty walled graveyard, quaint winding streets, half-timbered buildings, and elegant houses stretching away from the Common. We have quality tradesmen, excellent shops, top notch restaurants, theatres and tea rooms. We even have a copycat London arcade, but most importantly, John, this side of Oakbourne is jam-packed with doctors, solicitors, stockbrokers and surgeons.' And at least a third of those doctors, solicitors, stockbrokers and surgeons ran mistresses and second families which their wives didn't know about. Many smuggled prostitutes into their house, or visited brothels to indulge in vices that most working-class folk didn't have the imagination to invent.

'If you're suggesting my men have been asking in the wrong places, I assure you that's not the case. The higher up the social scale, the worse the clients treat the girls.' Collingwood's mouth twisted. 'The depths these women have to lower themselves to, just to eke out one more week, one more day, beggars belief.'

Faces flashed in front of her. Lily. Nellie Stern. Little Bridget, known to all and sundry as Birdie. Julia had thought — hoped — that she'd rescued them from the fate he'd described by inviting them to pose for risqué photos. Work that paid well and kept them out of the gutter. Oh, what they wouldn't give now for the chance to eke out one more week now, though. At whatever depths they might have to sink to...

'In fact, given the location of the body,' he continued, 'I'm inclined to think the killer's more likely to come from this side of the canal, that he has a deep hatred of women, and a problem in the hydraulics department.' Impotence often inciting fury and shame, he added, resulting in violence on a hideous scale. 'Jack the Ripper a perfect example.'

Julia picked up the glasses and bottle and beckoned him into her studio. 'I have no idea whether Rowena's killer —'

'Rowena?'

'Oh come on, I had to give her a name! She's been dehumanised enough as it is.' Julia switched on the light, revealing three washing lines at eye level, two of which were hung with photos pegged by one corner. 'The point is, whether the killer hates women or not, and whatever's happening in the hydraulic department, the motive for this murder isn't sexual. I'll show you.'

Collingwood's nose wrinkled. 'There's certainly nothing sexual about the stink in this room. What in God's name is it?'

'Gardenias. Don't ask.'

'I'm trying to imagine the man who commissions a portrait in front of Her Majesty's battleship, smelling more like Her Majesty herself. You were saying?'

'Half the men who come in by themselves wear hired clothing or uniforms, wanting portraits in front of backdrops that allow them to pretend they're someone they're not.' *Admirals, generals, clergy, toffs.* 'But back to Rowena, she was hit from behind, in other words, caught completely off guard.'

'So she wouldn't put up a fight.'

'Maybe. But my money's on her attacker not wanting to look her in the eye when he killed her.'

'I'm still going with him wanting no resistance when it came to undressing her.' Collingwood tapped the photographs with his index finger. 'The only time men take trophies, in this case clothes, is when the motive is of a sexual nature, and I won't tell you what they do with those clothes.'

Julia thought of what the collectors did with their postcards.

'So what's this, then?' Detective inspectors aren't the only ones who know how to point.

'A hatpin.'

'Exactly. And how big are ladies' hats, John?'

'Most street walkers wear modest arrangements on their head for, uh, practical purposes.'

Julia refilled their glasses, conscious that this was her fourth shot tonight, but who's counting. Then she told him point blank he couldn't have it both ways. If Rowena was a common prostitute, she wouldn't be wearing lavender silk, as per the fragments found under the body. But since she was wearing silk, it followed that she'd have an enormous hat piled with feathers like everyone else. She was also about to draw his attention to a whole host of other contradictions when he leaned down and pressed his lips against hers.

'Have I ever told you how arousing it is,' he said when he eventually came up for air, 'when you plant your hands on your hips like a fishwife to make your case?'

Replying would have been easier without his tongue in her mouth, but Julia had no desire to talk. Her desire was to run her hands through his hair, claw her nails down his back, and arch her back under his strong, naked body. She took his hands and cupped them over her breasts.

Three minutes later, he was kicking the bedroom door shut behind him, her in his arms, their breath was coming in gasps, and for a little while, anyway, everything was right with the world.

Collingwood couldn't help whistling as he left Julia's. He'd missed this. Only a month, but God, how he'd missed this! Not the love making so much, though he'd be a liar if he didn't say his heart bounced every time he pictured Julia naked — as did the hydraulic department. In fact, Earth would be a duller planet without the McAllister breasts railing against their tailored confines as she set her usual cracking pace along the street, skirts swishing, hat feathers bouncing. He chuckled. Jesus, he'd only just left her bed and the dough was rising again.

It wasn't that he'd missed the intimacy, either, in those four weeks, although that was another factor that had been totally lacking in his marriage. The warmth of contentment that comes from openness and sharing, of not being judged, but instead being comfortable in one's own vulnerability. True, Julia manipulated him last time round, exploiting her sensuality to wheedle information out of him. Did he blame her? Did he hell. He'd made it abundantly clear that she was his prime suspect, even before the body count started to rise. Who wouldn't use whatever resources were available to prove their innocence? He was angry when he found out. Obviously. His pride was more than a little hurt, too. But blame? Never. He respected her too much for that.

Collingwood turned into the Square, past what Julia called the Copycat Arcade, where moonlight danced on the glass, saluting to the night watchman checking the locks. Julia was right. This face of Oakbourne was a far cry from the other side of the canal, where the winding alleys would be teeming with hostile drunks and belligerent whores, where dazed customers would reel out of the opium dens, heading for homes where anxious wives would be waiting, and — this was the pitiful part — where children living rough, as young as six or seven, would be raiding the rubbish piles at the ends of the lanes in search of scraps before the rats got to them, or else picking out rags and bones to sell in the morning in exchange for a slice of bread or a kipper.

Collingwood moved aside for a hansom cab and found himself drawn to the hypnotic clop-clop-clop over cobbles. He was surprised how even the acid tang of the horse couldn't eclipse Julia's fresh citrus fragrance.

Had two old ladies not been snoring away at the other end of Julia's corridor (he really must ask her about that), he'd have stayed and watched the sun rise on her face. Buried his hands in her thick, dark hair and taken her until there was no breath left in his body. Luckily, that was a joy to look forward to, and look forward to it he most certainly did. What he'd missed — missed desperately — was that with Julia he could be himself. Not a powerless father. Not a reviled husband. Not the boss to whom two sergeants and sixteen constables saluted every time they clapped eyes on him, or certainly not the man answerable for every damned crime from fraud to murder to picking pockets in Boot Street's jurisdiction.

With Julia, he was John Collingwood, pure and simple.

Passing beneath a spluttering gas light, he grinned. *Simple, yes. But pure...?*

The whistling and sensation of the cat that got the cream lasted right until he rounded the corner into Thorne Road, then a vice clamped round his throat. With every measured step along this row of oh-so-respectable terraced houses, the screw turned and the grip tightened. By the time he'd reached the end house, he was barely able to breathe.

He braced himself.

Every curtain in the Collingwood house would be drawn. Not because it was the wee small hours. The curtains shut the evil out. The curtains were never opened.

He'd be facing total darkness inside, too, because light, unless absolutely necessary, encouraged sins to breed. It was never the blackness, though, that made his stomach churn. It was the silence. The house — the home — the building he'd inherited from his father, where a little girl once skipped and danced, sang and giggled, had become a house of death. No, worse. A living coffin. Emily had removed the pendulums from the clocks, effectively stopping time to allow Alice to heal. She'd covered the mirrors, arguing that, in such situations, vanity is a sin.

Emily was sick, too. He understood that, but she was the mother of his child, for God's sake. Deranged by the same grief and powerlessness that made him want Alice to be put out of her misery. In their different ways, both parents wanted the same thing. The best for their daughter. How could he deny his wife that?

As he approached the gate, his footsteps slowed. Worse than the crushing silence were the times when it was broken. Broken by recriminations. By the wheezing of ever weakening lungs. By the coughing, the spewing, the watery discharge, and the endless murmur of prayers.

So, as he unlatched the gate, Collingwood thought he knew exactly what he was facing.

He was wrong. On his doorstep stood the cadaverous frame of Sgt. Charlie Kincaid. Older than Collingwood by just a few years, the experiences of an earlier career in the Army had left their mark in a face that was rugged to the point of haggard. They'd taken Kincaid's left ear and two fingers as souvenirs, as well, but in all the time he'd been stationed at Boot Street,

Collingwood had never seen him with an expression that made the Grim Reaper look chirpy.

'It's two-thirty in the morning, Charlie. Wife kicked you out again?'

Ordinarily, Collingwood would expect a cheery riposte. Something along the lines of 'No, sir, she wanted to punish me for dropping her favourite teapot, so she invited her mother to stay', or offer a quip about this doorstep being softer than his mattress at home.

'I'm so sorry, sir.'

'Alice.' Collingwood could barely rasp out her name. 'She's passed, hasn't she?'

Kincaid nodded. 'I'm sorry, truly I am. She was a smashing little kid.'

Collingwood's knees buckled. 'Months, Charlie. Months I'd been praying for an end to her suffering.'

*Be careful what you wish for*, his mother would caution. His mother was wise, because suddenly the void had become unimaginably dark. The pain was like nothing Collingwood had ever known.

Most times when he looked in, Alice had been sleeping, and lately, even when she was awake, she would be too weak to speak. He'd still hold her, though. Rock her in his arms, tell her how much Daddy loved her, what they'd do when she was better, how so very proud he was of his baby girl, and try not to let his tears dampen her pillow. Now, the next time he'd be holding her would be the last, and this time she'd be cold. Never again would she light the room with her smile.

'That's ... not why you're here, is it?'

Collingwood fell back against the gate, because even though the father in him was fighting to come to terms with the loss, the policeman in him was putting the fractured pieces together. A house that was unnaturally quiet after a death. No doctors, no neighbours, not a flicker of light. Cognac rose in his throat.

'It's your wife, sir.'

'Christ, no. No, Charlie, not her as well.'

Suddenly the weeks, the months, when he'd avoided going home at all costs — anything to dodge the bitterness, the accusations, the church groups, the praying, the powerlessness of not being able to make his child better, the guilt at wanting her free of her burden — popped like bubbles. He was an idiot. A fool. He'd thought that, with work, with drink, with women, especially Julia, a man could forget. Pretend yesterday, today and tomorrow didn't exist. Engulfed in whisky or sex, he could live for the moment, and if putting villains in prison balanced it out, then surely the rest of his life would fall into place?

Now his family had paid the price for his arrogance.

A cat yowled on the roof, and he jumped.

'No. Mrs. Collingwood's alive.'

'What, then —? Oh, God, she took an overdose of laudanum, didn't she!' It's what she'd slipped Alice, to help her sleep. 'She was troubled, Charlie. Her mind had warped with the worry, but — the hospital. I have to go to the hospital. I need to be with her.'

Despite everything, she was his wife, She'd need him now more than ever before. He'd failed his daughter, he would not fail her, too.

A restraining hand fell on his shoulder. 'She's not in the hospital, son.'

Years as a colour sergeant barking out orders, along with a fondness for pipe tobacco and porter, had roughened Kincaid's voice to gravel. Never, though, had Collingwood heard it as rough as tonight. Never before had Kincaid called him son.

'She's at Boot Street.' Kincaid paused. 'Charged with poisoning your daughter with arsenic.'

# Chapter 7

The driver of the horseless carriage that had slewed off the road and prevented Julia catching her train should count himself lucky. The instant he realised it was heading for the tracks, he'd dived out, slithering ignominiously, but without injury, down the bank. His motor-vehicle, though, fared considerably worse — it was reduced to a tangle of twisted metal, torn leather and spinning spokes. It had also mangled the rails. Having assessed the damage, the experts from the Railway Inspectorate proclaimed it would be tomorrow at the earliest before trains were running again. And then probably the afternoon.

Julia was oddly relieved. Itching as she was to escape the ghosts that haunted her, bury the heartbreak that was tearing her apart, and dodge the hangman's noose, here was the first ever chance to show how crime scene photography might turn the tables on criminal investigations. It didn't seem right to walk away, leaving Rowena high and dry, and possibly scuppering any chance of the process being adopted in law. Another twenty-four, even thirty-six hours gave Julia time to finish developing the negatives, make plenty of prints and complete her list of observations before outlining her conclusions to Inspector Three-Times-a-Night Collingwood — preferably over an encore.

'Jaysus, I hope that Whitmore feller has a voice like goose down.'

*Damn.* With everything else going on, Julia had forgotten about her interview with the young Irish reporter.

'Out with me friends last night, I was. Too much milk stout, just between you and me. Well, didn't I wake up with the chronics this mornin'!'

'If you'd rather postpone until tomorrow —'

When Orla shook her head, black curls flew everywhere, as did the flowers on her hat. 'Yer don't think I'm putting myself through this kind of pain twice? Moind, I'm that hungry right now, I could eat the twelve Apostles and still have room for Mary Magdalene.'

'Then you're in luck.' Thanks to the piece Orla sold to the *Chronicle*, the French sisters had been swamped with so many donations from neighbours vying to out-do one another, the old ducks didn't know what to do with the stuff. 'Help yourself.'

Off came Orla's hat and in went a fork. Game pies, boiled ham, lunch tongue, cold beef. *Good grief*, Julia thought, *this girl could stand behind a lamp post at the best of times and disappear. Where on earth did she put it?*

'Tell me about Sam Whitmore,' Orla said between mouthfuls.

What could Julia say? That when his portrait was in the window passers-by mistook him for Buffalo Bill, after the American brought his Wild West show to London for the Queen's Jubilee? He had the same long hair, goatee beard, knowing look. That she had been fourteen and living rough when Sam took her under his wing, then taught her the business inside and out? That she hadn't known what to call herself back in those days, being on the run, and so Sam had called her JJ, which was neither a boy's name nor a girl's, but one which put her on equal footing with both, proving anyone can be anything they set out to be, providing they want it enough.

That he was the father she never had, and when he died, she was utterly lost? That he left everything to her, which she hadn't expected, and she had been running the business for the past four years under the pretext that he was still alive?

Or that, with one exception, Sam Whitmore was the only person she'd ever trusted, and look how that exception turned out...

'Wouldn't you rather interview the old ladies?'

Orla dismissed the notion with a large chunk of Stilton. 'Interviewed to death, them, which is why I wanted your slant yesterday. It's Sam Whitmore who gets my juices goin'. Gimme some background, will yer?'

Julia poured tea. 'Actually, I have a confession to make. There won't be any interview this morning.' *Sincerity is everything. Fake that, and you're fine.* 'His father was taken ill.'

'Has he gone far?'

'Edinburgh.'

The reporter's pencil hovered over her notebook. 'So basically, what yer telling me, Julia — I can call you that, can't I? — is that *you* took them photos of the crime scene yesterday.' Orla shot her a sharp sideways glance. ''Cause the way I see it, either the poor soul's wearing his feet out, walking to Edinburgh ... or he took a train before the lines closed.'

There were no flies on Orla Keane, then. 'My secret is out.'

'Yer shouldn't be ashamed of being successful, yer know.' Orla slapped a slice of ham on a lemon tart, which was odd, but strangely appealing. 'Word wouldda got out eventually, you having to testify in the courts and all that. In fact, with you leading the way in this new technology —'

'Assuming it takes off.'

'Repeat, with you leading the way in this field, yer might want to think about joining us.'

'Us?'

'The National Union of Women's Suffrage Societies. We're committed to giving women back the right to vote. Profile like yours can move the cause forward at lightnin' pace. Tell me you'll at least think about joining?'

Julia could just see the headlines. *Votes For Murderesses!* Thousands would flock to the banner. 'I'll think about it,' she lied.

'Can I look at yer pictures, then?'

'No.'

'Ach, come on. They're only back there, what harm can it do? If I'd been at the grisly scene meself, I'd have —'

'Trampled all over it, destroyed vital evidence, trashed any clues and made it next to impossible for the police to catch the killer.'

Orla chewed on a Bath bun. 'No means no, then?'

'No means absolutely, categorically not. And if I find you wheedling your way in, using an interview with the old ladies or indeed anything else as a pretext to look at the photographs, I will have you arrested for trespass and attempted burglary, understood?'

'Yer got me wrong, love. Them's the sort of tactics the men resort to, and didn't I tell yer I have to be forty times better?'

'You said twenty.'

'Ach, that was yesterday. It's two times harder today, but the thing yer should know is, I'm bigger than that. If I'm wanting something, Julia McAllister, I'll boggin well ask.' Orla grinned. 'Now I'm not saying I won't pester yer to the Colonies and back to get what I want, 'cause I will. But if yer say no and yer mean it, I'll respect that decision. There'll be no sneaky stuff on Orla Keane's watch, that there won't.' She looked at the cherry cake and decided there was still enough room. 'So come on, spill. What it's like to be Britain's first crime scene photographer?'

Of all the ways Collingwood imagined watching dawn break on Thursday morning, sitting in the hospital mortuary, cradling the lifeless body of his daughter, wasn't it.

Equally, of all the ways he'd imagined Alice dying, murder never entered his head.

At first, he was angry. Some zealous young medic, filling in for the family doctor, wanted to make a name for himself, did he? Desperate to have a paper in the *Lancet* or something, it was obvious he pounced on the first really sick patient he'd been assigned, refusing to accept this was a standard case of consumption, and went overboard with his diagnosis. Well, he could bloody well find another way to see his name up in lights. This was Alice the little oik was poking and prodding. *Get your filthy hands off my daughter.*

Then he met him and anger gave way to disgust. How could they send some incompetent pup to tend a terminally sick child? He didn't blame the locum for the misdiagnosis — it was not this poor sod's fault he was out of his depth. His name was Harrington. William Harrington. He was almost the same height as Collingwood, with a combination of sandy hair, gawky build and peach fuzz moustache that made him seem younger.

'Irregular pulse, thick coating on the tongue, pain in the abdomen, yellow skin, whites of the eyes conjunctival red —' Harrington recapped the symptoms.

'All consistent with a severe and prolonged illness,' Collingwood said.

'Absolutely.' Harrington held his gaze. 'For the same reason, you can argue that sore gums are to be expected when the patient's teeth aren't cleaned properly, and attribute numbness to too much time spent in bed. I'm older than I look, Inspector, and sharper than you give me credit for. Dr. Poulson was undoubtedly a competent practitioner, and having known the child's mother all her life, he would have had no reason to doubt her. But please understand, I know medicine, Inspector, and I know people as well. You, more than anyone, must see the importance of not taking statements at face value.'

Unlike Dr. Poulson, who'd been drip fed information, Harrington hadn't been swayed by the argument that a nurse wasn't necessary. 'It concerned me that Mrs. Collingwood remained strongly resistant to the idea, although this is not uncommon. There is often an unwillingness to hand over even the smallest role, inciting all manner of emotions. For instance, guilt at dereliction of parental duty. A mistrust of the incomer, are they capable enough, are they caring —'

Hitting too close to home, Collingwood's face burned with shame. 'You're suggesting it wasn't one factor, but an amalgam that made you look deeper?'

'I am suggesting nothing of the sort. Quite the opposite, in fact, and in any case, I am stating, Inspector, not suggesting. Concern, you see, immediately switched to alarm when I read back through the patient's notes. Dr. Poulson detailed very clearly how the child would rally almost to the point of recovery, then relapse.'

Finally, Collingwood forced his vision to focus on the wooden frame that was centre stage in this depressing airless room, with its ugly sink and ugly shelves, and stank of disinfectant. Forced himself to look at the wooden bars screwed crosswise into the frame, spaced precisely the optimum distance apart to support the cadaver, yet allow water from the metal spray tap hanging above it to drain into the hole beneath.

He'd seen this dozens, scores, hundreds of times, and it wasn't new, a white sheet covering a form that had barely substance, height, length or width. Boot Street's jurisdiction encompassed a number of rookeries and slums in which children met untimely ends, and where nothing but skin and bones lay under the sheet. But this was the first time his daughter's head had been supported by the wooden pillow that was a cross between a butcher's block and Madame Guillotine...

'Correct me if I'm wrong, Dr. Harrington, but isn't that also consistent with sufferers of tuberculosis? Their condition improves greatly, before the sweats and coughs kick in again, leaving them weaker than ever?'

'It happens.'

'Isn't it also true that patients with severe illnesses are more prone to contracting other diseases?'

'In my experience, more patients die of those than their original illness.'

'And if, say, one of those patients contracts food poisoning or some other gastric unpleasantness, would you agree that it's far from unusual for them to succumb to vomiting and diarrhoea?'

'Absolutely.' Harrington didn't blink. 'But I would be negligent in my duty to both my patient and my calling if I didn't take samples to be certain.' The experiment he'd carried out, he explained, was a basic test for the presence of heavy metals in the body, and the test proved positive.

Again, it was easy for Collingwood to punch holes in Harrington's argument. Since the test wasn't for arsenic specifically, surely one would expect to find traces of heavy metals, given that nitrate of bismuth was prescribed to counter the diarrhoea?'

'Precisely why I sent further samples to one of the finest forensic analysts in the country. A man who studied for many years under Dr. Alfred Swaine Taylor —'

'Professor of Medical Jurisprudence at Guy's Hospital.' One of Britain's foremost forensic toxicologists. The name was hardly unfamiliar to Collingwood. But this was his daughter. His wife. The mother of his child.

The tension in the doctor's chin softened. 'Listen, I know this is hard for you to accept, but the analyst has conducted several tests, and the results are the same every time. Arsenic poisoning.'

Collingwood shook his head. Emily had doted on that child. 'You can't be certain of that. Over the course of my career, I've had more than my fair share of run-ins with poison, and I'm familiar with these tests, Dr. Harrington. The Marsh test. The Reinsch test. They need time and study under laboratory conditions, and my daughter only died a few hours ago.'

'I know, and I'm really sorry, Inspector. I can only guess at the pain you're experiencing right now, but my suspicions were aroused several days ago. In fact, almost from the moment I stood in for Dr. Poulson. Which was why I took stool, urine and vomit samples, which all tested positive for high levels of arsenic. Now, before you point out that hundreds of households keep small stocks of the stuff to eliminate rats, yours included, the clincher was the crystal residue I found in the food Mrs. Collingwood prepared, and fed, to your daughter.'

Not only was it notoriously difficult to dissolve, arsenic was dyed indigo by the chemists, so there could be no confusion in the kitchen with sugar or salt. No confusion at all.

Collingwood didn't know what time the doctor left, or how long he'd been rocking Alice in his arms, telling her how much he loved her, how proud he was of his little chicken, how much joy she'd put into an otherwise joyless life. He recounted the times he'd given her piggybacks. The board games they'd played. The dolls he had bought her. The toy theatre they'd built together. He remembered the wide smile on her little face every Christmas, seeing the stocking hung over the fire heavy and bulging. The way she played with her pet rabbit, the inexplicably named Bluebell. The awe with which she watched women on bicycles, and the trembling lip when she was told she couldn't have one, much less a bloomer suit. The swift uplift of mood when he whisked a new bonnet from behind his back.

Vaguely, he was aware of sunrise in the mortuary. Of light glinting on the glass jars and bottles lining the shelves, and on the rows of metal instruments used for post mortems. He was aware of hospital sounds outside the room, too. Of the clatters and rattles of breakfast trolleys and bed pans, that the smell of boiled cabbage was competing with the stench of disinfectant — but these were otherworldly experiences that didn't impact on his life, any more than the *drip-drip-drip* of the tap in the sink, or the trill of a blackbird outside the window.

A father has one job, and one job only: to protect his child.

Tuberculosis is a pernicious but determined advocate of equality. It doesn't confine itself to the poor or the sexes, the old or unfit. It's purely the luck of the draw who wins and who loses the race. God knows, there were times when he'd considered holding a pillow over Alice's face when she was out cold, sedated with laudanum. End her torture, and the hell with the consequences. His role was to wrap Alice in the arms of his protection, and if that meant her finding peace at his expense, then they could hang him sixty times over, it would be worth it.

But this? Prolonging the suffering, adding to the torment...?

As a father, he should have been there for her. As a policeman, he should have been aware of what had been happening. Put a stop to it, before it became too late —

'You need to lay her down now, Inspector.'

Harrington's voice didn't reach him. It was the gentle shake on his shoulder. Slowly, his glazed eyes came into focus.

'Your daughter. You need to put her back on the table.'

Collingwood looked into the earnest green eyes of the doctor, then down at the girl in his arms.

Christ. He hadn't even noticed rigor mortis had set in.

# Chapter 8

Thankfully, most of us haven't witnessed the after-effects of a house fire. It's not pretty. At the best of times, the sisters' house was tiny, cluttered and cramped. Now, floral wallpaper hung off in charred sections. Paint and varnish had peeled away in long strips. Most of the furniture could be mistaken for charcoal.

'We'll pay you, of course.'

'Full rates, naturally.'

'But if you could take photos before the builders start work, we'd be ever so grateful.'

'We'll forget, see.'

'We know roughly what we had, and approximately where we'd put it, but once we sign the form for The Man From The Insurance, the workmen move in and...'

For the first time, leastways in public, the sisters burst into tears.

'You'll think us stupid —'

'— it's so silly —'

'— only there wasn't anyone else we could ask.'

'She means trust.'

'The idea of someone else recording a rummage through our belongings —'

'Too dire to contemplate.'

*Stop, stop, stop.* Julia was getting dizzy. 'I don't think it's silly, and I don't think you're stupid.'

From one careless act, these women had lost their home, their furniture and all their possessions, and were living off charity in a complete stranger's house. Whose brains wouldn't be addled?

'I needed to test out my new box camera anyway.' Quick fix, cheap fix, ideal for the purpose. 'Come along!' Besides, she'd never photographed fire damage before. Looking at it, though, it was a miracle the old girls got out alive. Half the ceilings had collapsed, any remaining floors a mere handful of boards, the whole lot mixed with an impenetrable tangle of water pipes, twisted by the flames to bursting point, and wires from an electricity supply that had only been installed in the autumn.

It wasn't purely the smell of smoke that choked Julia's throat as she captured the scenes on her roll of film. Cracked mirrors. Shattered glass. Floors covered with exploding knickknacks and china, or lumps of melted metal that were once teapots and cheap costume jewellery. Picture frames blackened and at odd angles hung on the walls, but without any artwork inside them. The inconsistencies were astonishing. Why had some treads on the staircase burned through, and not others? How come the metal wires for the stained glass in the windows were twisted, yet the glass didn't fall out? Why were the doors to the welsh dresser fine, when the contents inside had been fried? How is it you can have gaping holes in the ceiling, and the chandelier is untouched? Why had the chintz curtain on the left burned, while the right was merely shrivelled and black?

Next door's cat, a small tabby, poked a wary face round the door, sniffed twice and duly retreated.

'I'm going upstairs,' Julia said.

'It's too dangerous,' the sisters chorused.

'The average fireman weighs twice what I do — if they can manage it, so can I.'

'Then we're coming with you.'

'To make sure you're all right.'

Another banner headline for the intrepid Miss Keane. *Murderess saved by two sparrows!* If the situation wasn't so tragic, Julia would have laughed.

'That's a smart little camera, dear, if you don't mind my saying.'

After years and years of very basic designs, the concept of photography had suddenly taken flight and now hundreds, literally hundreds, of advertisements were popping up in the *British Journal Photographic Almanac* alone. Which is probably why, when an American named George Eastman came up with the idea of customers putting a hundred exposures on a single roll of sensitised paper, he also came up with a trade name that was novel, distinctive and universally remembered. Kodak. He came up with a clever slogan, as well. *You press the button — we do the rest.*

Julia's box camera wasn't a pre-loaded Kodak, which you posted off to be returned, fully loaded and with the old film developed. She'd used one of those to flush out the sick, twisted individual who'd murdered her models and tried to frame her, and threw it away afterwards. Too many memories. Too much pain. But to take off without a camera was out of the question, hence her joining the ranks of amateur button-pushers. This one was light, portable, did away with any need for tripods and plates, but...

'The problem,' she told the sisters, 'is there's no way to adjust the focus. On top of that, the aperture of the lens is very small and —' They were already lost. She changed tack. 'Basically, cameras like these work best in bright daylight situations but on the bright side, the subject matter isn't moving, so nothing can slip out of focus. I think they'll come out well enough.'

You'd expect books in the bookcase to act like kindling to the flames, but their very density had the opposite effect, giving the impression that Julia could almost pick one out and leaf through, even though they'd fused together. The velvet armchair in the corner where the fire had started was merely sooty, and totally at odds with the mattress and bedcovers, where only a twisted metal frame testified to this having been a bedroom at all. Again, the top half of the chest of drawers was ruined, whereas the lower drawers looked perfectly serviceable — assuming you could reach them for the rubble over what was left of the floor. Any rugs that remained were a crumpled mess glued together by heat.

'You do realise this will take more than a week to put right?' Julia said, stepping carefully from one joist to another.

The old girls clung to each other and nodded.

'If there's anything to salvage,' she added, 'I suggest now's a good time.'

There'd be no one to help them tomorrow.

'I don't think there's anything left,' the younger one quavered.

The clothes in the wardrobe were gone, as indeed was any kind of fabric, clothing or linens, and hat boxes were paraffin to the flames.

'Odd, isn't it, how some pieces escaped completely unscathed?' the older sister said wistfully.

'Like wildfires on the heath,' the little one said, 'this one jumped, too.'

'Either that, or we had a ghost without knowing it.'

A shaking hand patted the high backed chair upholstered in damask and gold that had been left incongruously untouched in the middle of the room.

'I doubt ghosts go to the trouble of protecting chairs, sweetheart.'

Watching them stifle their tears, Julia thought, regardless of what had escaped the inferno or had not, the trouble was every single item was sodden from the water thrown on the flames.

The old dears had lost the lot.

# Chapter 9

'Thank you ever so, Mrs. McAllister.' The butcher's daughter blushed. 'I mean, the way you took that picture so's people can't see my baby on the way!'

Julia picked an imaginary paperclip off the floor to hide her smile, and thought, *you might not see it in the wedding photo, but there's no mistaking her condition now.*

'And that one of me, me mum and me sisters, oh, it's lovely.' The woman held the framed portrait to her lips and planted a loud kiss on the glass. 'Perfect!'

'I'm sorry the one of you and your father didn't turn out so well.'

'He moved on purpose every time you tried to take it, the rotten pig. Mind, you should've heard him when I told him I was expecting. Thought he'd explode, honest I did and then, when I said we was having a white wedding —! White wedding, my — I won't tell you his exact words, but it rhymes with glass, so I told him, for Gawd's sake, Dad, the father's Billy White, so it's a white wedding whichever way you look at it.' She rolled her pretty eyes. 'Families, Mrs. McAllister. Who'd have 'em, eh?'

In a flash, Julia was transported to a Cornish mining village. Framed in the picture was a handsome miner and his wife, their two children scampering round the tiny cottage that went with the father's job. There was a little dog. A mongrel. And a kitten that the mother brought home for the daughter's seventh birthday.

Turning the page, the picture changes. This time, it's the mother's birthday, and to celebrate she's prepared a rabbit supper with a lovely apple crumble and a jar of elderflower wine. When the husband doesn't come home from shift, she's curious, but not concerned. He was always a one for romantic gestures, was her George. Perhaps he went picking flowers on the cliff?

The picture darkens. Men come. They're dirty, like the daughter's father when he comes home from work, and they smell of mines, like him. They've brought something with them in a barrow. Something heavy, that made them puff and wheeze, and some of them have white lines running from their eyes, right down their cheeks, like something washed the muck away in streaks. The little girl can't see what's in the barrow, because it's covered in a sheet that's stained with red, but there are feet sticking out the end. Wearing boots that look exactly like her father's.

'It's —' Julia cleared her throat. 'It's a beautiful wedding dress, Mrs. White.' Too many these days look like the wretched cake, but truly, hers was gorgeous. 'The fresh flowers sewn in to the bodice set it off.'

'Aaah, thank you, that was my idea.' This time the blush was pleasure, not embarrassment. 'Me mum offered me her dress, despite the rotten things me dad said, but me, I wanted something light and floaty. And you know what my Billy said, when he saw me coming down the aisle? Said he thought he was looking at an angel, and that's when I said, if it's a girl I'm carrying, then Angel's what we'll call her. What do you think, Mrs. McAllister?'

What Mrs. McAllister thought was that the loser in this game was the bride's father, being the only person in the church who couldn't see the love in these two youngsters' hearts. What she said was, 'I look forward to taking Angel's christening portrait.'

'Oooooh, come here.' The new bride wrapped Julia a hug that would put the average bear to shame. 'You've done us proud, me and Billy, that you have. I'm so grateful to you. In fact.' She turned in the doorway. 'I'll get my mum to drop some pigs trotters off tomorrow, and a nice bit of lamb's liver for the next day.'

The silence after the door closed was like the inside of a tomb, only thicker.

Would Julia miss this life? Of course. Photography by its very nature is intended to bring pleasure, commemorating the very best things in people's lives. Sometimes, of course — a good many times, in truth — the portraits were of loved ones who had passed, and these, admittedly, were not so easy. Often they were lying in their coffin, but it wasn't unusual for Julia to have to prop up the deceased in a chair and have his or her picture taken surrounded by the family. Even then, tragic though the circumstances were, this was often the only picture they would have of the departed. It might not make them happy, but it gave them comfort.

But at times like this, Julia's mind always found its way back to that little mining village. To the tall, handsome man who clocked off with black dust choking in his throat, head pounding from twelve hours spent drilling out the rock, every organ in his body reeling from the blasting in the tunnels. The same tall, handsome man who was so dog tired that he missed his step. The effects on a human being after dropping a hundred feet down a mine shaft are horrific, but amazingly, it doesn't always result in mortality. At least not straight away. Without exception, though, every man who had survived wished that they had not.

So while, in that respect, Julia's father was lucky that Death claimed him instantly, fortune didn't favour his widow in quite the same way. Her son wouldn't qualify for work underground for another three years, and though women and children were employed on the surface, pushing trolleys and breaking up the ore to a size manageable for the crusher, the family's combined income was still too low to cover the rent on the tied cottage, never mind food and fuel. Faced with the workhouse or the only man who offered his hand in marriage, she bound herself to him — unaware that she'd done a deal with the Devil.

Julia's mother had discovered, too late, that his principal activities were drinking, violence, and biblical quotes delivered at the end of a fist, a belt, or that pathetic appendage he considered his manhood.

Julia might miss Whitmore Photographic, and Oakbourne, and making peoples' faces light up, but putting together a compendium of contrasting cultures, showing the majesty of nature and capturing scenery guaranteed to make eyes pop out on stalks isn't exactly the short straw.

The gallows, on the other hand. That's the short straw.

# Chapter 10

Even though it was an American term, Julia still called them Derby hats, because that's what Sam used to call them. He'd travelled extensively in the days when plates needed developing within ten minutes of taking the photograph and being on the other side of the Atlantic when these hats became fashionable, he'd stuck with the American name. A few times, in those early times on the road with him, Julia and Sam would debate whether it was called after the famous horse race or the Earl of Derby, who'd popularised the style. They never did get to the bottom of that one but calling them Derbies was her way of keeping Sam with her.

On the other hand, the camel felt monstrosity whose brim was touched when its owner entered her shop didn't deserve such an accolade. It was a bowler hat, and an ugly one at that. It also immediately identified him as a plain clothes policeman.

'Miss.'

He looked uncomfortable, but whether that was due to the preponderance of fragile items dotted round the premises, always a worry for tall men, or the cut of his brown corduroy suit only time would tell.

'DS Kincaid.' He showed her a card confirming that warrant number 2863 had indeed been issued to one Detective Sgt. Charles Henry Kincaid, who joined the Oakbourne police on the 4th April, 1880. 'Boot Street.'

*Well, well.* 'I presume you're here about the Apollo Theatre murder?' Julia's wide smile said, *What other reason could there be?* The trickle of sweat down her backbone said, *I'd feel much happier if there was a back door to this place.*

'The Inspector asked if you wouldn't mind sharing your findings with me.'

Julia froze. This wasn't right. Why would Collingwood send a minion? He'd left in the wee small hours with a grin you'd have to chisel off, insisting the old proverb was absolutely right — it was better to give than to receive, and she'd better brace herself when he called round later, he was in a very giving mood.

She took a closer look at the warrant card before handing it back. Everything was perfectly in order. She must shake this cynical business of always thinking the worst. 'My pleasure, Sergeant. This way.'

A nicer person would have offered him a cup of Darjeeling and a cream bun to go with it, but nice people don't kill other people then bury them in unmarked graves. Julia set a brisk pace to her studio, where the photos hung like grisly bunting on the line.

'Guns.'

'Excuse me?' She'd obviously misheard.

'She'll look good with guns.'

The penny dropped. Of course Collingwood didn't delegate any minions to stand in for him. The warrant card was either forged or stolen, that ridiculous false voice should have warned her, and if there was any doubt about it, his awful suit and dreadful felt bowler were the clincher. It was a poor disguise, but adequate for fooling her into admitting him, and besides. She should have twigged that policemen, while mostly drawn from the lower sections of society and therefore generally haggard in appearance, still don't look like the Grim Reaper with a toothache.

Luckily, the studio was full of poles and stanchions for propping up her various backdrops. While he leaned to examine the first print drying on the line, Julia grabbed the nearest stick and swung it.

Rowena's killer was out cold before he hit the floor.

Julia was kneeling on her prisoner, tying him up, when there was a knock on the studio door.

'Sorry to interrupt, dear, can you spare a minute?'

'Is it urgent?' Julia was three-quarters of the way through trussing her prisoner like a chicken for the oven, and it would be nice to finish the job.

'The Man-From-The-Insurance is here. We'd really appreciate an impartial observer.'

'Give me two minutes,' Julia called.

Tall and wiry, he was still heavy, and now he was starting to come round. She tied a scarf round his mouth as a gag, and would take great pleasure later telling him what use her models had put that scarf to.

She brushed her hands, checked the knots and, satisfied the chicken wasn't going anywhere, joined Mitzi and Minzi or whatever their names were in the parlour. They didn't need her, of course. They didn't need anyone, this was a straightforward claim. But while they'd done well to hide their distress at the sight of their burnt-out possessions, this was a harrowing experience for anyone, never mind two women in the twilight of life.

In the doorway, Julia paused to take in the scene, to capture it in her memory, the way she'd photographed the old ladies' home for them, because after today, memory was all it would be.

The little clock on the mantelpiece, flanked by the white jade vases Sam had picked up in Peking, during the aftermath of the Opium Wars. Symbols not only of freedom of religion in

China — the right to evangelise, as it was sanctimoniously called but the legalising of the opium trade, opening the door to misery for millions of British, European and American citizens, as well as giving British ships the right to carry underpaid indentured Chinese labourers to the United States. Who could imagine two elegant vases could stand for so much misfortune?

Her eyes moved on to the curly antelope horns he'd brought back from Africa, pinned to a board that hung next to the mirror. The inlaid oval dining table, currently covered with a tablecloth, cups, saucers and a rack of sandwiches, meat paste by the looks of it, where she and Sam had laughed and played chess and got drunk and shared every last damned secret. The frames on the walls in which most people hung paintings, but where she'd mounted Sam's photographs of the American Civil War. Hardly comfortable viewing, but that was the point.

She was jolted back by a nasal whine saying, 'Need I remind you, ladies, I'm a busy man. Let's knuckle down to business, shall we?'

Stuck with this pair for longer than ten minutes, the Man-From-The-Insurance would have had every ounce of Julia's sympathy, poor bugger … had he bothered to lift his nose out of the file.

'And you, sir, are —?'

'Oh.' He jumped at the vision in lemon and lime who'd swept in behind where he was sitting. 'Turrow, Harold Turrow from Griffin Insurance.' Julia and Turrow shook hands. 'A niece, I imagine?'

'No, Mr. Turrow, this is my house, my studio, my shop, the French sisters are my guests and while they're staying here, I'd be obliged if you would at least pretend to be interested in their plight.'

She'd seen him before, but for the life of her, she couldn't place where. Not a portrait. She'd have remembered the challenge of photographing balding and ginger, especially when they came with overly white skin and freckles. His visiting card showed Griffin's offices were on the Square. That didn't narrow it down.

'Yes. Well.' He coughed away the admonishment. 'If you could just sign here, ladies —'

As one, the old dears leaned forward, their faded blue eyes peering at him over the little round spectacles balanced at the end of their noses.

'What are we signing?'

'We need to know what.'

'The settlement. Here's a pen —' Turrow said.

'You mean our claim is wrapped up?'

'Already?'

'Rely on the Griffin,' he said, quoting the company's slogan with the enthusiasm of a comatose drunk. 'Pen, now, ladies.'

Julia took a step forward. Half-lion, half-eagle, griffins were the guardians of riches and treasure. 'Shouldn't they read it first?'

'No need, no need. This is merely an agreement binding both parties upon which to proceed until the forms can be typed up and posted for signature.'

His language was equally mongrel. Half English and half designed to confuse.

'Then perhaps *you* should read it.' She took a seat opposite him, eye to eye, and folded her hands on the table. Where on earth did she recognise this man from? The loud check woollen suit refused to elicit any clues, neither did the dapper little boater. 'Aloud, if you wouldn't mind.'

With a sniff that made it clear he wasn't happy having his authority questioned, least of all by a woman, he picked up the agreement. 'I, Miss Elizabeth French, and I, Miss —'

'The gist will suffice.'

Pale eyes that reminded her of boiled gooseberries fixed themselves on the little rack of sandwiches. 'After careful consideration,' he said stiffly, 'Griffin Insurance have come to the conclusion that the terms of the policy have not been met and the company is not, therefore, liable.'

The old ladies shrieked.

'What!'

'We get nothing?'

'Fire is not listed among the named perils to be insured.' He made great play of consulting the policy document. 'Explosion, lightning, theft —'

'B-b-but the house bears a fire plaque of your own griffin!'

'Made of iron!'

'Those things.' Turrow snorted. 'After the establishment of municipal fire brigades, insurance companies ceased to be responsible for their own firefighting arrangements. With respect, madam, those old plaques are as obsolete as crinolines and sailing ships, and it is incumbent upon the householder to be aware of this.'

In other words, the fact that they took out a policy with Griffin Insurance, in the belief that the company's plaque on their wall meant they were covered as per the old days, was their problem, not his.

'Why didn't your company take it down, if Griffin were no longer responsible for extinguishing fires marked by their symbol?' the elder sister asked.

'You should have taken it away,' the younger one sobbed.

'I accept this must come as a disappointment to you, but if you could just sign here, here and here, and initial here, here and here, both of you, please, I'll be on my way.'

'You will indeed, Mr. Turrow,' Julia said sweetly. 'But there will be no signatures, no initials, and you can leave the agreement on the table where it is.' She stood up. 'The Misses French will be in touch with your offices shortly. Come. Allow me to show you out, Mr. Turrow.'

The only sound she could hear, after pulling down the shop blind and turning the Open sign to Closed, was the sound of the old ladies wailing.

# Chapter 11

'The Boss said you might be trouble.'

Julia felt the earth tilt sideways. Not because Rowena's killer had unravelled every knot, taken the string, rolled it neatly in a ball and placed it on the seat of the bicycle that leaned against the wall of her studio. Not because he'd folded the scarf that served as a gag, and draped it across the handlebars. Not even because he was sitting, one long leg slung over the other, in the big armchair used for portraits in which the patriarch of the family sat surrounded by his adoring (but standing) loved ones. But because the warrant card wasn't fake.

His ugly suit and uglier hat weren't some terrible disguise, any more than the voice was disguised to make it sound like he'd been gargling with bleach. This was indeed DS Charles Henry Kincaid, warrant number 2863, that she'd just slugged, gagged and tied up tighter than a string of onions. From here, Julia could see — unfortunately very clearly — the mangled remains of his left ear, while the hand that stuffed the pipe with tobacco from a soft, red leather pouch was most definitely a couple of fingers short of the full count.

Julia smoothed her skirts, fluffed her leg o'mutton sleeves, then did the only thing a girl can do at four o'clock in the afternoon in circumstances such as these. She reached for the forty-year old Courvoisier, still here from last night, and poured two generous measures.

'I'm more of a stout porter man myself, but I won't say no this once.'

'It's very good for headaches.'

'Well, that's a handy thing to know, but if it's all the same with you, Mrs. McAllister, I don't much fancy any more. The one you've given me will do very nicely for a while.'

'Yes... About that...' It took a second before Julia realised that wasn't rainwater gurgling down the metal drainpipe — that was the sound Sgt. Kincaid made when he laughed.

'Not sure I can arrest you for assaulting a police officer when there's no cuts or bruises, not even a witness to back up my claim.' He picked up his hat. 'Wilful damage to police property, on the other hand...'

'The least I can do is buy you a new one.' She would be doing the world a favour.

'No, no, not this.' He shot her a broad wink. 'It's precisely because of people like you that people like me need bowler hats. Hard as granite, see.' He tapped it against the arm of the chair. 'Designed for gamekeepers originally, did you know that? Tight fit, stops them blowing away in a gale, reinforced with resin to protect the game warden's noggin from low branches.'

'Not to mention female photographers with the wrong end of the stick, pun intended.'

There is was again. *Gurgle, gurgle, gurgle.*

'The test's to jump on it. If our trusty bowler keeps its shape, it's still up to the job when a man's out working the streets. Same reason I wear one of these.' He pulled down his collar to reveal a strong black leather band. 'Wore 'em in the army. Saved me from many an angry cutlass, this, only don't let on to Mrs. Kincaid that I still need it. She'd kill me with her own bare hands, if she found out the biggest threat to Robert Peel's finest is garrotting. Hard hats being no match for blunt instruments, in case you hadn't noticed.'

Julia shuddered. And to think she'd taken Collingwood's derby as a shallow show of fashion... 'I'm truly sorry I clouted you, Sergeant. It's just that when you said she'll look better with guns, I assumed you were the killer, bluffing your way in to take my photographs as both trophies and destroying any evidence linking you to the crime, while fantasising about other ways to kill.'

'Can't fault lightning fast reactions, Miss. My only regret is that Yours Truly was the recipient, and a tip for the future, by the way. Should you have the urge to tie up any more intruders, use sailors knots, and a variety of them. Took me less than two minutes to pick my way out, but the guns thing? I was talking about her.'

Kincaid nodded to the backdrop of how a local artist imagined the new HMS *Prince George* would look once she was in service, battling choppy seas and stroppy navies, flying her colours with pride.

'My nephew serves with the Channel Fleet, which this lovely lady will be joining once the work's complete. Only right now Madam's sitting in the water, waiting to be fitted out with forty-four guns of varying sizes, and a few torpedo tubes thrown in for good measure.' He drained his glass and stood up. 'But talking of killers...'

He tapped the close-ups of the victim's injuries with his pipe stem.

'Taking into account the passing of rigor, along with post mortem lividity — ah, sorry, Miss, that's the —'

'Discolouration of the skin from the pooling of blood. I know what that is.'

'Right. Well.' He tried to look comfortable with that admission of knowledge and failed. 'The pathologist puts the time of death some time on Monday, caused as a result of three blows to the back of the head, in his opinion part of a frenzied erotic assault.'

'Whatever that quack thinks, this is anything but a straightforward sex crime.'

'Never is, when killers fiddle with the bodies.'

'The killer didn't fiddle with the body. See here? Rowena's underclothes —'

'Rowena?' Kincaid interrupted.

'Since your mob haven't been able to put a name to her and murder's so degrading, I had to call her something that was unusual and at the same time dignified. It's the least she deserves. The point is, the killer stripped her of her outer clothes, but apart from being dragged around, her undergarments are completely intact.'

'Someone disturbed him halfway through? It's not unusual,' Kincaid said, or rather, rumbled. 'Punter picks up a prozzie, takes her to what he thinks is a quiet, secluded location, because what he has in mind isn't your run-of-the-mill wham-bam-thank-you-ma'am. He kills her. Three hefty whacks to make sure. But then, just as he's starting to warm up to the reason he took her there in the first place — I dunno? kids, a couple of drunks, thieves looking to divvy up the spoils? — come along. Punter panics and runs off.'

'Taking a huge bundle of skirts, petticoats, hat, reticule, probably a parasol, with him. Without dropping a single kerchief or a shoe. Or anybody noticing.'

'Hm.' Kincaid rubbed his chin. 'You think this was how she was meant to be found?'

'What if she wasn't meant to be found at all? What if the killer thought a patch of waste ground behind a tumbledown theatre was so obscure, nobody would ever go there?'

Julia unpinned the prints from the line, took them in the kitchen and laid them across the table like the pieces of a jigsaw. While Kincaid scrutinised the prints, she made a fresh pot of tea and set out a selection of cream buns, lemon biscuits and an iced ginger cake.

'I don't think Rowena was a prostitute, either,' she said. 'How many ladies of the night wear drawers?'

'Fair point,' Kincaid said. 'But her underclothes are shabby, they're old, and they're patched, and to me that spells one step up from poverty.'

'You think she might have been reduced to turning tricks to pay the rent?'

'Factory worker, fired from the job and for whatever reason couldn't find another one. Shop worker, caught with her fingers in the till, word soon goes round when you're persona non grata in that line. Widowed suddenly, left without any means. Who knows? She's not in the first flush of youth, this one — mid to late thirties, at a guess.' He dunked a biscuit in his tea. 'Still. If your Rowena was new at this lark, maybe her first time on the game, she wouldn't know how the system works —'

'— and wouldn't be suspicious of going behind derelict theatres with a stranger.' Julia arranged the photographs on the table into a different pattern. 'What troubles me are these scraps of silk. Silk is expensive, totally at odds with the faded chemise and darned stockings. She was dragged around a lot in the process of being undressed, dead weights being notoriously hard to shift. But you can still make out how her hair was originally pinned in a chignon, and look at this — would a woman staring at the workhouse waste precious resources on cosmetics?'

Kincaid flipped back through his notes. 'You're right. The PM recorded traces of zinc oxide on the victim's face.'

The white powder that turned women's faces fashionably pale. Consumption chic, as Collingwood once called it. 'I'll bet your post mortem also turned up traces of antimony sulphide on the eyelids and mercuric sulphide on the lips.' In other words, all the tricks women used to make it appear that they were cosmetic free, when in fact they were plastered in the stuff. 'I remember smelling perfume at the crime scene.' And the only scent that lingers that long is expensive.

'Her teeth were anything but cared for.'

'Your Inspector implied her skin was work worn.' Julia reached into the dresser drawer for a magnifying glass. 'He's right. Look here. Her hands are rough and calloused.'

'Broken fingernails.' Kincaid leaned back, sighed and hooked one arm over the chair. 'On the outside, then, the lovely Rowena is a lady. Lavender silk. Elaborate hair-do. Fancy hat. Underneath, though, we find a very different woman.'

'That's what I was trying to tell your boss. Contradictions at every turn.' *One. Two. Three.* 'How is he, by the way? Everything all right?'

''Course, Miss. Why wouldn't it be?'

But something passed behind the sergeant's eyes. She saw it.

'Right, then, best be going.' Was it coincidence, him closing down the conversation when he still had half a cream bun on his plate? 'Thank you for the tea.' He indicated the jigsaw on the table. 'Are any of these ready to take back to Boot Street?'

'All of them.' Julia scooped them up. 'In fact, I'll go one better and put them in an envelope to save your inside pocket splitting, although I still have more plates to develop yet. They might shed light on some of the anomalies. Incidentally —'

'Miss?'

'If your hat came through unscathed, not to mention your skull, thank God, why did you bring up the subject of damaging police property?'

With a grunt, he reached into his waistcoat pocket and brought out his brass police whistle, bent in the middle at exactly forty-five degrees.

'I won't be pressing charges, though.' Kincaid shot what she was coming to discover was his signature wink. 'I reckon drinking on duty makes us even.'

As Julia let the sergeant out, an Irish tornado in bright red cotton swept past and made straight for the kitchen, saying, 'Well, now, is that fresh tea I can smell?' before plonking herself down at the table as though she owned the place.

'So come on, spill. What did Charlie Cod want?'

'Who?' Julia just about managed to swap the crockery before Orla had chance to gulp down Kincaid's cold tea. She was too late to save the half-eaten bun.

'The DS back there. I call him Charlie Cod, on account of the fish-eye stare he always gives me.' She rolled her big, dark eyes. 'Like he's God's gift to women! I tell yer, that face could drive rats from a barn.'

'Mr. Cod came to collect the crime scene photos.'

'Aw, no, don't tell me.' Orla piled her plate with flapjacks. 'He took the boggin lot?'

'He did.' Technically speaking, anyway. The plates yet to be developed didn't count.

'Darn and darnation, what I wouldn't give to take a peek at 'em.' Orla consoled herself with a pile of lemon biscuits. 'Did he talk about the case?'

'He did not.'

'But he thought the photos was a help?'

'He did.'

Orla scribbled that down in her reporter's book. 'Victim got a name?'

'Not yet.'

'Ach, come on, Julia.' She licked the tip of her pencil. 'Spare me the non-committal baloney. Tell me about the photos. Pleeeeease. Yer a photographer, you've got a good eye. Tell me what yer saw in 'em.'

'I saw a handsome woman cut down in the prime of her life.'

'I need more than that, and yer know it. This is me career I'm lookin' to make here. Story like this'll put me name in big gold letters, if I play me cards right. Have yer seen this afternoon's *Chronicle*?'

'Bit short of time.'

Orla reached into her bag and brought out a copy.

### BOOT STREET LEADS THE RACE!

*Inspector Collingwood has broken the mould by engaging Britain's first crime scene photographer! Copying Parisian detectives, he is employing, for the first time ever in this country...*

Extolling the virtues of the technology and the reasoning behind it, the article went on to outline other weapons in Boot Street's forensic artillery. The relatively recent standardising of mugshots, for instance, using no fewer than twenty-four set measurements to accurately record and identify criminals, from ears to hairlines to noses. (Another French advancement). The new use of paraffin wax and resin compounds to preserve footprints at the scene. (More French technology). And how dynamometers were now able to determine the amount of force used in breaking and entering. (What do you know, yet another French innovation).

The article finished by saying that the Metropolitan Police refused to comment on the use of crime of scene photography, other than to say they were following events very closely. And summed up by pointing out that this was the same Metropolitan Police who still hadn't found Jack the Ripper, despite their own rough attempts at the practice during that particular investigation, and who dismissed out of hand the notion of fingerprint identification, even though the Argentinian police had found it exceptionally effective and Charles Darwin's cousin spent ten years studying the concept, only to conclude that the chances of two people having the same fingerprint were one in, wait for it, sixty-four billion.

'Boggin good start, don't yer think?'

'Not if you ever want a job in the Met's jurisdiction.' Scotland Yard bent over backwards, trying to pin down the Ripper, investing in more pioneering technologies than most people imagined, including scientific study of the human mind to decipher the mental characteristics of not only this particular killer, but murderers in general. 'But yes, to answer your question, Miss Name in Gold Letters, it is a boggin good start.'

It was well researched without getting too technical, and, for a reporter, surprisingly supportive of the police. (Scotland Yard excepted).

'I need to build on it, moind. Move beyond the facts, flesh it out, and the best way to do that is with a picture in the next piece. Perhaps you standing outside the old Apollo —'

'In your dreams.'

'Standard portrait, then.'

'Orla, you can chase me to the Colonies and back a million times over, and you're still not putting my face in the paper.'

Admittedly, the odds of her stepfather's family in Cornwall seeing Julia's photo in the *Oakbourne Chronicle* were slim to non-existent. But if the Metropolitan Police found the odds of one in sixty-four billion too high, why should Julia risk it?

'Yer too modest, you. Wait till we get you at the Suffrage meetings! So then. If not a photo of yerself, how about one of the crime scene? All right, the victim? 'Cause we might not know who she is, poor cow, but you can bet yer last penny whistle there's some poor stook out there, pacing ruts in his livin' room, wondering why the wife hasn't come home. Has she left him? Had an accident? Been kidnapped for the white slave trade? Or a couple of bairns, starvin' to death alone in the house, too tiny to reach the door knob. Or —'

'Orla!'

'What? Facts is boring. It's people what makes the world go round, Julia, and it's people what gives a story it's kick. That's why I didn't drop by earlier. I was over in Bentley-on-Thames, you bin there?'

*Don't think about the mansions on the river. About drugs. Prostitution. Blackmail. Coercion. Don't think about death...*

'Course yer have, what a rope I am, even askin'. Just a hop down the line, it is, which reminds me. The Railway Inspectorate's been back. Reckon the London line'll take longer to fix than they thought, so they're running omnibuses between here and the next station up, on account of the kerfuffle it's causing.'

Julia wiped her sweating palms on her napkin, and prayed to God that the ghosts of the past wouldn't get wind of her new identity and follow.

'Anyways,' Orla was saying. 'Bentley-on-Thames. Posh town, posh houses, posh people. LOT of money lives there. Me point bein', there's this fella, see, convinced his stepmam killed his dad, when at least a hundred people saw the stepmam at the time the deadly deed was done. And here's what I mean about a story. There's this poor stook — well, not poor, he's actually filthy, stinking rich — found dead in his house, the place robbed to buggery, but the fella's son can't accept it's a simple burglary. Random acts of violence don't figure in his rarefied, entitled world, see. And with the servants having cast iron alibis, who else can he blame? Will that be brandy I can smell?'

In her rush to swap the dirty plates, Julia had missed Kincaid's glass.

'Don't tell me Charlie Cod's been knocking that back! And him on duty, too, the hypocritical — no, I won't say it, not in front of a lady.'

'It was the French sisters.'

Orla's little pointy nose wrinkled in disappointment. 'I'd heard they were fond of a dram o' Scottish water. Pity, 'cause I could have — Never mind. Where was I?'

'Wicked stepmothers.'

'Or not so wicked in this case. See, I've met her. Interviewed her a couple of times as a matter of fact, and the woman's devastated. Not about the son's ridiculous claim, I meant about the husband. Right torn up, she is, poor bitch, but the thing is, the son won't let it go. And that's the story, Julia. That's why people will read me piece when I'm finished, and that's why they'll remember it. The toll grief takes, twisting even the gentlest of human souls.'

# Chapter 12

With its two-foot-thick cob and granite walls, heavy thatched roof and roses round the door, the Royal Oak was the prettiest inn for miles. In winter, a crackling log fire seduced customers into staying far longer than they'd intended, and in the summer, during the lull between the sowing and the harvest, the landlord provided ample trestles and benches in the orchard at the back for folk to meet, drink and be merry.

The sign didn't come from the preponderance of oaks in the area, or even the little stream, the bourne, which, combined, gave Oakbourne its name. The pub commemorated an incident after the last battle of the English Civil War, when Prince Charles, his army outnumbered almost two to one, lost the Battle of Worcester, along with his bid for the crown and virtually all of his men, then found that escaping the Roundheads was quite a challenge when your hair is longer than a girl's and you stand 6'2" in stockinged feet. To his credit, he'd managed to cover forty miles before the net closed in and then, ignominious or not, he found a giant oak tree, and took refuge in its leafy camouflage for a whole day, before the soldiers gave up and it became safe for him to flee to France.

Did the public accept the Prince cowering in the branches as dishonour and defeat? Did they hell. They saw this as another step in Charles' defiance of the Puritans and loyalty to his Kingdom. The man was a hero, and when, nine years later, he finally reclaimed the crown, that many taverns were renamed the Royal Oak in celebration, it became the third most popular pub name in the country.

Where more appropriate for another man, beaten and humiliated, to hole up?

'You can't worship at the Temple of John Barleycorn for ever.' Kincaid set down one glass of stout porter, a glass of pale ale, along with two tumblers of whisky. 'Sooner or later, son, you'll have to go home.'

Collingwood snorted. 'When you turn the key in the lock tonight, Charlie, will your house be reeking of death and despair? Will there be empty spaces where uniformed officers have confiscated items as evidence? Will your wife be sitting in handcuffs, with a constable standing guard and a matron acting as a chaperone?'

'Better house arrest than a cell in Boot Street.'

They weren't on a bench in the orchard, among the merry throng. As with all men on the run, Collingwood kept his head down, his eyes lower, and found retreat came surprisingly easy in a snuggery with tiny windows that made the room dark, even in daylight.

'How long before the analyst's report is back?' he asked.

Kincaid shrugged, but not because he didn't know the answer. It was the shrug of a man who wished he was somewhere — anywhere — else. The shrug of a man who would turn back time, if he could, or wave a faerie wand and make everything right. The shrug of a man who wasn't accustomed to feeling helpless. 'Dr. Harrington says most likely tomorrow, possibly Friday, but if he can hang it out until Monday, he will.'

Collingwood chinked tumblers. 'I appreciate your keeping this under wraps, Charlie.'

Sooner or later, the top brass would find out that the daughter of one of their inspectors was dead, and that his own wife was the killer. Sooner or later, the public would find out, too, at which point Collingwood's whole world would explode. He just couldn't decide whether he wanted it to blow up now and get it over with, or later, verging on never. He stared at the cheap watercolours on the walls. Cheerful scenes, of wheatsheafs being stacked and cows in pasture. Happiness frozen in time, contentment in perpetuity. If the artist walked in now, he'd have him arrested for fraud.

'How did the crime scene photos turn out?'

'See for yourself.' Kincaid shook the contents of a thick envelope on the varnished wooden table.

'Mrs. McAllister give you any trouble?'

'If you mean, did she hit me on the head, tie me up and gag me...?'

That was the first time Collingwood had felt like smiling. He wasn't sure it made it the whole of the way, but it came bloody close. 'I rather meant about parting with her theories.'

'She was surprisingly keen to share them, as it happened.' Kincaid scratched his chin. 'Odd case, this, and no mistake. You sure you want to pursue it now?'

'Because it's seven o'clock at night and you're starving?'

'Me? I'm like a duck for foie gras.' He patted his stomach. 'Your crime scene photographer should call the place Whitmore Tea Rooms, and I'd be happy to sign off on a liquor licence, as well. That's one very fine brandy she serves up.'

'How about because it's seven o'clock and you want to go home to your wife?'

'I'm there so rarely, Clara's forgotten what I look like, and for that she's very grateful.'

Nothing fazed Kincaid, and Collingwood envied him. The things he'd seen during his stint in the Horseguards, the things he'd done, would leave a lesser man haunted, mistrustful, beset by nightmares and terrors. Not his sergeant. Kincaid rolled with the punches and came up smiling. Or what passed for smiling, on that craggy face.

'Good. Now that you and I have nowhere better to be, and nothing better we should be doing, I suggest we put our heads together and work out to catch this killer, before he adds another floozy to the list.'

'That's the point, though, isn't it, sir?' Kincaid slugged down the whisky and reached for his pint. 'Are we sure she's a floozy? The boys have trawled every inch of the red light district, they've asked round the rookeries and slums, talked to the barge people on the canal. Nothing.'

*Someone must be missing her. Why hadn't they reported it?*
'Unfortunately, we can't print any of these pictures in the press in the hope she'll be recognised. You'll just have to keep plugging away and widen the search.'

Collingwood had no idea how his future would pan out, but he was buggered if he'd end his stint at Boot Street, possibly his career, on an unsolved murder.

'Your police photographer has a theory about why Rowena — uh, the victim was struck three times from behind.' The sergeant separated out the photos of the head wounds. 'She thinks the first two whacks were hard enough to send her flying but not hard enough to kill her, which accounts for the broken fingernails and the dirt underneath them, as she scrabbled on the ground.'

'More than possible.'

'She also reckons the victim's hat cushioned the first two blows so in order to finish the job, the killer pulled it off, causing her hair to become dishevelled.' He pointed to one of the photos. 'If you find the hat, she said, you'll find blood inside, then you can trace who bought it from the milliner's label.'

*Top marks, Julia McAllister.*

'The offer still stands, sir.' Kincaid finished his beer and wiped his mouth with the back of his damaged hand. 'You're welcome to room with me and Clara, until this mess passes over.'

'I appreciate that, but...' Collingwood upended his glass, too. 'The Temple of John Barleycorn serves my religion very nicely for the moment.'

'Can I get you another prayer for the hymn book?'

'Go home, Charlie. Hug your wife, take both her hands in yours and tell her you love her. You have that rarest of treasures, a sound and happy marriage, and believe me, working all hours of the day and night is not the way to maintain that state of bliss.'

'Listen, if I followed your advice, Clara'd think it's 'cause I'm about to drop a bombshell, and the only reason I'm holding both her hands is so she can't hit me.'

'Just sod off, you silly bugger.' For his sins, Collingwood was laughing. 'See you in the morning, Charlie.'

'That you will, sir.'

In the dim light, Collingwood returned his sergeant's salute, leaned back against the snuggery's wall and looked across to the bar. To the vase of wild flowers picked this morning, wilting on the mantelpiece. The bell pull, from the days when you could ring for service. The landlord, pouring pale ale through a gurgling, slooshing air pump, while his customers discussed politics, cracked jokes, told lies, moaned about their bosses, their pay, their working conditions, their children, their wives and their health. None of them, he noticed, complained about never having to buy their daughters a birthday present ever again. Or what a relief it was, not having to hang stockings over the fire at Christmas any more. No whining about packing away tiny clothes. Or dolls. Or colouring books. Or the toy theatre they'd made together.

*Hug me, Daddy. Harder, harder. Like you did before I was sick...*

So help him, if he went home now, he wouldn't be able to stop himself from placing his hands round his wife's neck and crushing her throat.

With a heavy sigh, Collingwood switched on the electric light in the snuggery and examined the photos of the crime scene.

For some reason, people associate the fellows who wait for the chorus girls after the show as lowlifes, stalkers and perverts. Far from it. Stage door johnnies were universally educated, well turned-out, and not short of a bob or two, either, and the reason they were waiting was to escort the ladies on a pre-arranged dinner date.

Ira — Aaron Adelman as he was then — had no pre-arranged dinner date, but every night and every matinée, he'd sat glued to the same front row seat. In a provincial theatre, admittedly. Life on the road doesn't allow for detours to West End productions, but never underestimate the quality of small theatre performance, especially the Gaiety Girls. Few, if any, had actually worked at the Gaiety Theatre, but the concept had taken the country by storm, with the term coming to symbolise the elegant, fashionable, demure young women who danced in the chorus of wholesome musical comedies. In short, Gaiety Girls were today's ideal modern woman.

And when the girl at the end of the chorus line smiled at him two performances in a row, he didn't just cancel appointments to catch every show, he was emboldened to do something he'd never done in his life: send her flowers. For that, of course, he needed her name. Gigi? Oh, my. Theatrical, bold, exotic, all at the same. How exciting! He starting sending bigger, more expensive bouquets, then perfume, until finally he could contain himself no longer and sent her the pride of his jewellery collection. A little dragonfly brooch studded with rubies, diamonds and sapphires.

A smile twisted his lip. He was a jeweller back then, and a good one. He had status. Class. He fitted in well with the stage door johnnies.

The smile dropped. Ten years had passed since Gigi stepped through the door in a blaze of lavender silk...

Standing in the shadows across from the Oakbourne Theatre, he watched the line of cabbies pat their horses, debate the news, smoke a cigarette.

At last, the stage door opened.

*Gigi, my love, my darling, my sweet.*

# Chapter 13

'Here's the roll of film recording the damage to your house.' Julia handed it carefully to the old ladies. 'Make sure you keep it away from the light, especially when you send it off to be developed. And here's the finished portrait.'

'Ooh, that's lovely.'

'Such a pretty frame!'

'Is it silver?'

'It shines beautifully.'

*Tweet, tweet, tweet — remind me never to keep birds.*

'And the backdrop!'

'What a handsome steamer.'

'Steamer? Silly me, I thought it was a battleship.'

'You're so kind, Mrs. McAllister.' A tiny claw clutched at Julia's wrist. 'How much do we owe you?'

'My pleasure.'

'No, no, no, we must pay for the frame.'

'I won't hear of it.' It would only tarnish in the window after Julia had gone.

'We forgot to thank you for being with us to meet the Man-From-The-Insurance.'

'Means so much, dear.'

Where had Julia seen Turrow before? All day it had been niggling away at her. To quote Orla, he might not be God's gift to women, but people you pass in the street rarely stick in the memory, no matter how unprepossessing.

'Why did you ask him to leave the form, dear?'

'She didn't *ask*, she told him.'

'She did, now you mention it.'

'Can we —?' Julia scaled back on the exasperation. 'Can we discuss this in the morning?'

*I'd heard they were fond of a dram o' Scottish water.* Dram? Julia could smell it a mile off, and there were already two empty bottles under the sink. No wonder the sisters' place went up like tinder. The entire contents were probably impregnated every time they breathed out. But it was right that they didn't sign the insurance agreement. Harold Turrow had been quick to draw up a settlement of zero. Too quick, some might say.

*Tap-tap-tap.*

'There's only one inspector who'd be knocking this time of night — Good God, who are you? And what have you done with Inspector Collingwood?' Face grey. Clenched jaw. Eyes hollow, with dark circles beneath them. And was that really stubble on his chin and creases in that oh-so-suave lounge suit? 'You look terrible.'

She expected him to roll his eyes at her lame joke, or say, flattery will get you nowhere, or, better still, crush his lips to hers.

'Long night,' he said instead. 'Longer day. I wonder if I might trouble you to discuss the scene of crime photos with me?'

It was not so much the voice that turned him into a stranger, more the manner in which he was speaking, as though he didn't know her at all.

'Talk to me, John. What's happened? Is it —'

She put her hand on his arm. He didn't exactly brush it away, but reaching inside his jacket for the envelope had the same effect.

'You've already given us a first rate female perspective on this case.' He laid the photographs on the counter like playing cards. 'And once again, my deepest apologies for the lateness of the hour, but like all murders, time is of the essence. So if I could pick your brains a little further, I'd be grateful.'

Her stomach clenched. *He knows.* God help her, he'd found out about her stepfather. It was the only reason he would be so distant. She clenched her fists behind her back. *Breathe in. Now breathe out. Don't throw up. But he needs something before he arrests me. He needs ... what? Information! Yes, that's it. The photos.*

'My pleasure.'

There was something wrong with Julia's legs. The bones had disappeared, her knees were nothing but jelly. All the same, she managed to walk to the window on feet that didn't betray her. He couldn't see the hands that shook when she moved the blind to peer round.

'Expecting a visitor, Mrs. McAllister?'

'Not at all.' *Just checking for police constables loitering in doorways.* 'Just checking to see if it's raining.' *Coast clear.* 'Cognac?'

'Tea.'

*No please. No thank you. Just one word. Tea. She was going to be sick.* 'Let's take the pictures into the parlour,' she managed to croak. 'The light's better.'

More importantly, it allowed her a better chance to escape, and as he gathered them up, she thanked God and all the angels in heaven for remembering to grease the lock two days ago. The key made no sound when she unlocked the shop door.

So then. Coast clear. Escape route open. Satchel and carpet bag handy in the dark room. All you need to do is distract him, grab your things and run like the Devil. The same Devil you killed, and thought you had buried...

'I've been thinking about the anomalies, and I've come up with four possible solutions.'

'Only four, Inspector? You must be slipping.'

There it was. A half-smile, revealing a glimpse of the man she'd taken to her bed, and who in turn had taken her in many other places besides. Situations like that — when you breathe in the same air they've just breathed out, when the taste of their skin lingers on your tongue, when you let them see parts of you that no one else has seen and she didn't mean physical — you think you know someone, then Julia remembered. Delicious as the experience was, the reason she seduced him in the first place was to pump him for information about the bastard who'd killed her models and was framing her for the crime.

'I'm holding up four fingers,' she managed to trill. 'Start ticking off the possibilities.'

Was Collingwood really that underhanded? That ambitious? In the parlour light, he looked ten years older, and Christ, if he didn't want that bloody drink, she did. This was killing her.

'The victim could be a kept woman,' he said, unaware, or perhaps uncaring, that the teacups were full of cognac. 'No money of her own explains the tired underwear.'

Julia stopped pouring. Dear God, was that how the system worked? Mistresses kept penniless to keep them compliant? Pictures filled her head. Of women, empty and alone. Everything bought for them — food, clothes, rent — but nowhere to go, nowhere to run, because they didn't have the funds. Women who were not physically abused, but victims all the same. Exactly like her mother. Thousands of them. Millions of them. Tied to a monster, either by marriage or emotional kidnap, at their wit's end and terrified. Terrified of the future and the work house that awaited...

'A man doesn't kill because he's bored with the mistress,' she said in a voice that was commendably even.

'Uh-uh.' He sipped absently. 'More likely she threatened to tell his wife of the affair, or go to his superiors.' There were many occupations where that sort of thing could ruin a man, he added. Should word get out.

'Well, you know what they say, Inspector. No point in having double standards, if you don't live up to both.'

'You're the one who mentioned the two faces of Oakbourne, and the Boot Street beat has its fair share of judges, bishops and magistrates, to name but a few.'

Under different circumstances, Julia would have relished the image of the bishop, mitre wobbling precariously, as he legged it down the street with a bundle of bloodied women's clothing in his arms. 'What's the second option?'

'A widower — nice tea, by the way. Any chance of a second cup?'

Another glimpse. Or another pretence?

'It's not uncommon,' he was saying, and there she was again, thanking God and all those sweet little angels that he couldn't see the trickle of sweat snaking its way down her spine. 'A man becomes so grief-stricken, and grows so desperate that he pays a prostitute —'

'I thought we'd agreed she wasn't on the game.'

'You and Charlie might have.' He shot her a sharp look. 'The whole purpose of my job is not taking things at face value ... look, let's not talk about that right now. The point is, our widower persuades "a woman" to imitate his late wife, right down to having her dress in the dead woman's clothes.'

Actually, it sounded rather comforting. Having "her" with him again, and now Julia thought about it, she could see lots of lonely widowers following that pattern. It's just that the picture she saw was more of old men seeking companionship, than younger ones wanting sex. Which is not to say older men didn't. Or weren't capable of bashing heads in.

'So he takes her to a secluded location where they won't be seen, with the intention of making love to his dead wife one more time.' Julia felt the pain of these poor, unhappy men. 'Clearly he didn't follow through and, overcome with shame, you think he killed the substitute to obliterate any trace of what he saw as a hideous betrayal of his wife?'

'Explains why he took the clothes.'

The uncertainty was driving her mad. *How did he find out? Had the Devil's body turned up? For God's sake, what gave her away?*

'If that is what happened here,' Collingwood said, 'it means the murder is a one-off, and unless he walks into the station and confesses, we'll never catch him. He could be anybody.'

In theory, the police could whittle down a list of widowers in Oakbourne. In theory, they could question every man on the list about where they were on that particular Monday, ask them to provide a detailed description of their wife, age, height, weight, can they take a look at her belongings, please, is there a photograph they might show them, to verify their story, then check their alibis. In theory.

In practice, Boot Street, didn't have the resources to carry out such an investigation. For that matter, what police station did? True, if this was another Jack the Ripper case, they would draft in extra officers and go round knocking on doors, asking questions, following up. Along with riots and the like, that was the whole purpose of police reservists, and equally, if this killing was the only crime committed in Oakbourne this year, there would be no problem in assigning every man to the case.

Except Oakbourne straddled the Southolt arm of the Grand Union Canal, making it one of the busiest sections of waterway west of central London. How many barge owners and deck hands passed through? Thousands. How many had lost their wives? Oh, yes, thousands. These people didn't have access to the same medical facilities, that the "nice" face of this town had. In fact, they didn't have access to medical facilities full stop. More of these itinerant women died in childbirth than God should ever allow, and since they worked alongside their men on the boats, they were susceptible to all manner of accident and disease.

Add on the dark slums on the factory side of the town, where strangers sleep six or more to a room and have to grope their way up dark stairwells with their hand, the temptation for crime is too great. Men get robbed for a penny. Women are raped. Children, too. A stupid brawl, one that no one even remembers how it started, all too often ends at the hilt of a knife. Houses are burgled. Funds embezzled. Poisoners feed their victims with a spoon and a smile.

'Rowena,' Julia said.

'Huh?'

'If the killer's not caught, that's not even the name she'll be buried with. She'll end up in a pauper's grave without a headstone. Nobody will find her, nobody will know who she really was, and no one will ever have the chance to shed tears and lay flowers over her.' *This is why you hang for the crime.*

The Trevellicks would see her hanged like a shot. Unlike Julia's father who came from a family of tin miners, they were fishermen, from the opposite coast of Cornwall. Sadly, those weren't the only differences. Without exception, they were brutish and coarse, traits that were alien to Julia's bloodline, but which ran through generation after generation of Trevellicks, and included the women and children. Briefly, she'd considered them suspects behind the framing of her for the models' murders, since no grudge was too small, no

100

memory too short, and certainly no vengeance too cruel. But only briefly. Cunning and sly, they weren't thinkers or planners, and subtlety didn't enter their heads. Also, twelve years had passed, when even her own mother wouldn't recognise the woman Julia saw when she looked in the mirror.

The point being, her stepfather might well have been court-martialled out of the army, after serving three years in military prison for violent conduct and not learning his lesson. But he was part of that family, and therefore cherished. That they were all drunkards and louts didn't matter. Like attracts like, and for twelve years, the Trevillicks had lived with uncertainty. As it happened, he'd gone off many times without warning, a trait the-Julia-in-a-previous-life seized on, and who knows? Perhaps they were the way they were because the life of a fisherman is bloody damn hard, and too many are lost at sea with no gravestone.

*Two wrongs still don't make a right.*

'Good looking woman,' Collingwood said, rolling the tea cup slowly between his hands. 'It bothers me why no one's reported her missing. Surely someone, somewhere, must be wondering where she is?'

Could he hear her heart pound?

'Another tragic consequence of poverty?' Julia asked. 'No one cares?'

The biscuit tin was stuffed to overflowing with florentines, fig rolls and gingernuts, the cake tin with Dundee, iced buns and almond cakes. Hardly the right accompaniment to mop up Napoleon's finest, but faced between putting the police between herself and her escape route, they would have to bloody well do.

'Theory number three?'

'Similar to theory number two, but instead of a widower, we're looking for some bast uh, blackguard who meets a woman, buys her clothes, and to very exact specifications, I suspect, because he wants to recreate ... I don't know, a lost love? When push comes to shove, though, he's unable to follow through with his erotic fantasy. Perhaps she laughs at him, perhaps she tells him how dare he, she's not that sort of a girl, perhaps she simply doesn't live up to the dream, but that's it. Before he knows it, she's dead, and for whatever reason, maybe he stole them from where he works, the murder will be traced back to him through that particular set of clothing.'

The colour was returning to his cheeks. The eyes less sunken. The look behind them just that little bit less haunted. For a split second, just a fraction, she caught something behind the grey eyes of the wolf suggesting he might be the hunted, rather than the hunter.

'None of those scenarios fit with the location,' she said, shaking off the feeling.

Collingwood frowned, and the moment was lost for ever. 'How so?'

'In all three instances, you have to ask why here?' Julia tapped the derelict building in the background of the photo. 'If a widower, a fantasist, or a blackmail victim wants to pretend it never happened, why leave her in the open?' He'd come here for a purpose, she pointed out. That mission hadn't been accomplished. Why not put the remaining time to better use and literally bury the past? 'In short, why risk having his victim found, when he wasn't pressed for time?'

'Which brings us to the fourth and final possibility.'

In the distance, the bells of St. Oswald's chimed midnight. Owls would be flying, foxes would be foraging, small creatures would be scuttling through the undergrowth at the edge of the churchyard, and corrupt sextons would be digging up freshly buried corpses to sell to the anatomists.

Was that really so dreadful? Modern medicine advances as a result, the dead are past caring, their loved ones none the wiser, because what you don't know doesn't hurt you? Bloody right it was dreadful. The breach of trust was so far north of appalling that it threatened to overtake itself as it circled back round the earth. A contract had been entered into, one in which the dead rested in peace. Without ethics, how could society hope to survive?

*The sun shall be turned into darkness, and the moon into blood...*

Did Julia lose sleep about killing the Devil? Not a wink. Call it hypocrisy, call it a different set of ethics, but in the space of just a few years, the violence had escalated to the point where he was one fist away from killing her mother and brother. Julia, of course, got off relatively lightly when it came to knuckles and buckles. The bastard saved other weapons for her.

'What possibility would that be?' she asked Collingwood.

'The man who wants to kill the same person over and over. Scotland Yard had such a case, as did the Birmingham police. In both instances, the killers wanted to murder their mothers. If the killers can be believed, the things these women did to them when they were very young boys turns even the most hardened of stomachs.'

'Just my opinion.' Julia reached for a florentine. Caught a whiff of something that wasn't *Hammam Bouquet*, more like stale perspiration. 'But if Rowena looked like his mother, then she must have given birth very young, making him nineteen, twenty at the most.'

'Boys younger than that go off to war, and believe me, Julia, those boys know how to kill.'

'Do they know how to undress their victims to the extent that every trace of top clothing is removed? Would a youth think to remove gloves? To take their shoes? Would they even think about women wearing such things in the first place?'

'Female perspective,' he said, crunching into a gingernut. 'See what I mean? You know, we'd have made a good team, had the circumstances been diff— Anyway.' He stopped slouching and became Detective Inspector Collingwood again. 'You reckon our killer is an older man, who isn't fixated on his mother? Who, though?' he wondered. 'A wife? A sister? The girl who jilted him at the altar and made a fool out of him?'

*If the circumstances had been different? Why the past tense, John?*

'God knows,' Collingwood continued, 'but one thing's for sure. He will do it again.'

'Not necessarily.' *Keep it going, keep it going, don't let him know you suspect.* 'Suppose this was his first time, and he stopped because the act of killing wasn't like he expected. The smell of blood, and the sight of brains and splinters of bone made him sick to his stomach?' *Keep trying, keep talking, make him relax again.* 'Or,' she pressed on, 'he realised he'd made a mistake, she wasn't a prostitute, and that's why he left?'

*Collingwood almost gave himself away back there, and he knows it. But it's midnight, he's drunk, he's tired, but most importantly he's at odds with his conscience, that's why he's dishevelled. Work on that, then distract him, grab your bags and run. Play it right, and you'll have a good ten minute start.*

'Possibly, but if this is his motive for murder, pound to a penny, he'll strike again, or he wouldn't have had the presence of mind to undress her.'

'Naturally, he'll need to steel himself for the job. Bolster his own confidence, put himself in the right frame of mind. But make no mistake, he will strike again, and the next prostitute he hires? He'll want her to dress in exactly the same clothes. That's why he took them. He has a compulsion to recreate whoever it is he needs to kill.'

'First thing in the morning, I'll get Charlie to ask around. See if anyone's asked for quality clothes to be mended. Of course, if our culprit is wealthy, he'll live in a large house and arrange for one of the servants do it, then we'll never know.'

'Highly unlikely he'll do that.' *Tell him there are more prints in the studio, he ought to take a look. That one of them holds an important clue. Then tell him you need the lavatory. That you'll join him in just a few minutes...* 'No man is going to encourage gossip in his own household by asking one of the staff to mend a dirty torn and bloodstained dress,' she said. 'Trust me, if he wants it mended, he will contact a professional seamstress.'

'Excellent.' He stood up and looked more like the man Julia knew. The man Julia knew, and suddenly feared. 'As always, I appreciate your help and co-operation.' He strode to the door. 'I never thought of it as adultery, you know. It was never that simple.'

With that, he picked up his hat and was gone.

# Chapter 14

'Sorry, love.' The lock keeper turned the windlass like he was turning air. 'Rozzer asked me the same question a couple of days ago, and me answer to you's the same as it was to him. Might've seen her. Then again might not.' He shot Julia a mischievous grin over his shoulder. 'Under them great big Quaker caps, all barge gals look alike.'

That wasn't true. The stiff, heavy bonnets worn by every woman who worked the narrow boats, even children, differed a great deal. Some were so white they made your eyes water, others were pink mauve, or cornflower blue, some were pastel, others vivid, some used floral fabric, others plain. They were as varied as the ladies who wore them. Each, though, had been lovingly crafted with the neatest tucks and most skilful pleats right the way round, boasting veils, like a nun's, to protect their necks from the sun. They were designed round face shapes, to make them as flattering as possible, which meant most were fetching in the extreme.

On the other hand, Julia knew what he meant. Four thousand miles of canals linked their way round Britain, and the days of bargees living static lives while their children went to school went so far back that the dinosaurs lost count. Call it progress, but to compete with the railways, whose routes were already treble that of the waterways, bargees had been forced into an itinerant lifestyle, taking whatever cargo they could find to whatever destination was required. Scores of locks were unmanned, the job of opening and closing them falling to any children on board, so any time they were staffed, people tended to remember the lock keeper. A beacon of light on an otherwise dull and slender highway. The man to whom the boatmen could exchange banter and cheery hellos, and tips about what lay ahead. He, on the other hand, would need a memory like an elephant to remember a fraction of the hundreds — the thousands — who passed through. Not to mention an inclination to do so.

'Actually, that wasn't the question.' Julia watched the water swirl as the sluice gates opened. 'When I gave you her description, I didn't ask if you saw her the other day.'

'No?' The lock keeper put his back to the bar and pushed.

'My question was, had anyone asked if you'd seen her during the past few days. One of the boat people, perhaps?'

If Julia could at least put a name to the victim in what little time she had left in Oakbourne, it was a start.

'Wish I could help, but I can't.' His weather-beaten face wrinkled in apology. 'Friend o' yours, is she, this woman you're looking for?'

'Yes.' Just not in a way he'd understand.

He nodded to the captain of the narrow boat edging into the lock. The barge lined up in front of it was red and green, the one behind blue and yellow, this barge just happened to be a glossy bottle green, with white and gold trim. But all of them, from the doors to the water can to the buckets, even the plaques on the side, were decorated with garish roses and fairy-tale castles with red roofs, pennants, turrets and bridges, the lot, as though Bavaria had somehow exploded over the canal, dragging the Brothers Grimm with it.

As the sun warmed the air, creating a smoggy haze over the factories and swallowing the chimneys, the photographer in her noted the decorative rope work and distinctive white lettering on the side of the boats. As with the flowers and castles, it was another means of binding displaced individuals into a community that transcended their nomadic existence. Like the women in their distinctive bonnets and the men in their waistcoats and caps, every barge boasted fancy lacework at the windows, sending out a message out loud and clear — and that message said kinship.

What Julia wouldn't give for even a tiny fraction of that.

'Try the lock at the Southolt end. If anyone knows what's going on round here, love, it's his missus.' The lock keeper pulled the sort of face you usually see in the music halls. 'Busiest body this side of St. Paul's, and the nosiest parker this side of Big Ben.'

'Thanks.'

Along the tow path, she stepped aside for a small boy, seven, maybe eight, leading a big black blinkered Shire horse, its harness glinting with brasses. Fewer and fewer barges were horse-drawn these days, but steam or horse, nearly all were loaded with coal. Did the injustice of it stick in the boat people's throats? Here they were, carrying food for the very machines that forced them into this nomadic life in the first place? Or did they weigh the advantages of a family living and working together as a team, with no ties, against the lower pay of the factories whose furnaces they fed and whose inmates had no life outside work and the pub?

The big question, Julia supposed, is would they go back to the way things were in the past? Would anybody, for that matter?

The lock keeper was right. Mrs. BusybodyNosyParker did know everything that went on around here. She knew the blond boy who worked the winch at the refinery was having it away with the cooper's wife and the coalman's daughter at the same time. That the magistrate with the big nose kept a secret Chinese mistress. That the boot maker on Cadogan Street was going out of business, having drunk away the profits. And the owner of the Welsh dairy was going blind, and him only forty-seven, poor soul.

Unfortunately for Julia, Mrs. BNP didn't take the slightest interest in the "dirty scum" who plied the canal, despite the fact that if it wasn't for them, her husband wouldn't have a living and she wouldn't have a roof over her head. For all her vast local knowledge, though, Mrs. BNP didn't recognise Rowena from Julia's description, or know of anyone who'd been asking, apart from that police constable, though she had it on good authority that he was up to his ears in debt from a gambling, too. Rat baiting, so she'd heard.

Julia wasn't beaten yet.

Like every town sliced by a canal, crime was higher than the national average. This wasn't because the boat people were brawlers, killers or thieves, despite what Mrs. BNP thought. (Although like every community, they had their fair share). It's just that once the railways became the focal point of the industrial revolution, people were thrown closer together than ever before, and while the factories paid more than agricultural work, the further people move away from nature, the more hardened inside they become. Few bothered with church any more. Most probably couldn't quote the Commandments they broke every day, much less the Seven Deadly Sins they committed nigh on every hour.

Musical halls sprang up like weeds to ensure disposable income was invested their way, but they were no match for public houses, and with the Demon Drink came all manner of unseemly behaviour. Some of it ended in pounding hangovers, some in the cells overnight, some being sacked from their jobs — and there are only so many times a man can be fired before he becomes unemployable.

Equally unemployable was the repugnantly high number of men, women, even children, injured during the course of their work. True, some of the factories paid compensation, but as a rule the amounts were pitiful — and when you've lost the use of both hands, you can't work.

However you end up there, though, unemployable invariably means living rough on the streets. Unemployable invariably means turning to crime. Crime that includes prostitution, for men, women and, sadly, children too. Had Rowena been forced to turn tricks so her children didn't have to?

Julia wasn't convinced she'd been on the game, at least not in the traditional sense, but Collingwood's theories wouldn't stop buzzing round in her head. The mistress, kept penniless to keep her compliant, who'd reached the end of her tether and threatened to go to her benefactor's superiors. The widower, yearning for his lost love and hiring a substitute wife. The jilted bridegroom taking revenge. The man who kills the "same woman" over and over. At the time (was it really only last night?), she'd been panicking, so only part of her mind was on Rowena.

*I never thought of it as adultery, you know. It was never that simple.*

With hindsight, Collingwood being so distant and formal made sense, and explained the stubble and the crumpled suit. He'd worried himself into the ground not wanting to hurt her, when he — how could she put this? — terminated their arrangement. *Really, John? You don't know me very well, do you.*

Perhaps it was his ego. Perhaps it was every man's ego? That they take a girl to bed and expect the girl to fall for them. *Well, sorry to disappoint you, Inspector. I like you. What we had was entertaining and utterly delicious, but that's all it was. A distraction for me, a diversion for you, and very nice it was, too. Love, though? Stick to detecting, Inspector.*

It was bloody quick work, though. Finding a replacement for his passions. She hadn't taken him for the type, but Collingwood must have been cosying up to his new woman well before he left Julia in the early hours of yesterday morning, whistling and muttering about repeating the experiment with the feather boa —

*Wait. There is no replacement, you silly cow.* That wasn't the behaviour of a man who's juggling two mistresses, quite the opposite. There was only one explanation for that hangdog expression, the odd formality, the distance he put between them and, most tellingly of all, his unkempt appearance. He'd pledged fidelity to his wife. Unhappily married or not, he was re-committing himself to the union.

*I never thought of it as adultery, you know. It was never that simple.*

Collingwood's wife told him on their wedding night that if he had to assuage his filthy desires, she wouldn't stop him, it was his right under marriage, but not to expect her to participate. No amount of cuddling and coaxing could change her mind, so he'd sought release through the triple conduits of whisky, women and work, and soon discovered he excelled at all three.

Until, Julia thought, Death stared Alice in the face.

Collingwood had done a deal with the Devil. He had nothing to lose by sticking to his vows — only his daughter to gain.

*According to my wife, the consumption is my fault. Apparently the sins I investigate stick to me, and it's that evil, coming into the house and accumulating, that's causing my daughter's illness. Since she won't listen to reason and I won't resign from the police force, my wife spends every waking moment praying for God to make Alice better.*

He couldn't quit his job, but it looked like fidelity, in other words celibacy, was the compromise they'd agreed upon. No wonder the poor bugger looked haggard.

And shame on her, too, Julia should have known better. Had Collingwood known about her own deal with the Devil, he'd have challenged her about it, heard her out, or (and admittedly this was wishful thinking) at least warned her. She'd jumped to conclusions, because she was edgy after the murders of her models and being framed for it, then the bitterest of betrayals that cut into her soul, and because starting a new life was at the forefront of her mind. When you're scared, you don't think straight, and all she could think of last night was that she'd come too far to let the Devil win now.

'Good morning, sorry to trouble you.'

The man from the slop shop eyed Aaron warily. 'If you're selling, I ain't buying.'

'I'm kicking.' Tailor slang for looking for a job. Aaron had picked this from when he was a boy, watching his father make shirts and swearing he'd never follow that backbreaking route.

'How long you been on the board?' The man meant, how experienced.

'Been on the baby since I was a baby myself.'

The man grunted. 'I'll ask the cork.'

For five minutes, maybe longer, Aaron stared at the door that had closed in his face. Should he knock again? Take the hint? Slop sellers weren't renowned for their geniality. They churned out ready-made clothes by the ton on the cheap. Time was money, and time was short. He ran the Fedora round and round in his hands. Put it on. Took it off. Found his foot wouldn't stop tapping the step. Finally, the door opened and a different head poked out.

'I need a baster,' the boss said, 'can you do that?'

'I can cover every —'

'This is skiffle work, mate. To make it pay, stock's gotta move fast. I got cutters, I got buttonholers, I got machinists, I got pressers, and them what presses waistcoats don't press trousers, in fact I got twenty-odd sub-divisions going on. Now can you baste or can't you?'

'I can baste.'

'Eight bob a week, including Sundays.'

*Eight shillings? That was nothing short of slave labour!* 'Sounds fair.'

'Seven in the morning until eleven at night.'

'Six till ten.'

'Seven till eleven.'

'Six till ten, it's the same number of hours.'

'And I open same time each morning. Yes or no?'

'I'll think about it.'

'Not here you won't, you've wasted enough bleedin' time. Knock again, and you'll be wearing your nose on the back of your head.'

He should have said yes. Basting was easy work, long stitches tacking the garments together, and it was a miracle he'd found this place, to begin with. He thought he'd covered them all. Had to pinch himself when he discovered another tailoring shop that wasn't owned by Jews. Was it too late to apologise and take up the offer?

Aaron's hand hesitated over the shiny brass knocker. Slop shop owners aren't famous for soft hearts and tender outpourings of emotion. It's dog eat dog in that industry, with the ready-made market a nice juicy bone. He'd break Aaron's nose as soon as look at him. A man's reputation is everything in that game.

He should have said yes. Only ... last night, watching the girls spill out the stage door, remembering what it was like. That heady moment, standing on the precipice, when he'd said, 'Can

I buy you dinner?'

Was it so wrong, wanting to relive that first night?

He retraced his steps down the narrow lane behind the factories. The air was thick with smoke belching out from the chimneys, beggars whined on the corner, delivery boys wheeled barrows as fast as they could, heedless of shins that got in the way, but all he could think of was Gigi, resplendent in lavender silk.

They might be chorus girls, but the ability to sing wasn't remotely important. A choir behind the scenes, or sometimes in the wings, took care of that. Gaiety Girls just had to be pretty, lithe, respectable and demure — and, of course, have shapely legs. Indeed, some vulgar louts even went so far as to call these musical comedies "leg shows".

Aaron Adelman, as he had been then, wasn't vulgar. Aaron Adelman lived in the stratosphere and was a maestro with gems. He made band rings studded with diamonds and sapphires. He fashioned floral diamond pendants, and dazzling tiaras, and only ever used the finest quality jewels. Diamonds from India, sapphires from Montana, Russian emeralds and Afghan rubies. He didn't cut the gems himself, but chose the cut stones for their strong play of light, be they rose cut, pear cut, or triangular. A skill that culminated in the production of an exquisite dragonfly brooch studded with rubies, diamonds and sapphires, the pièce de resistance of his collection.

Nothing less for the girl who smiled at him. The girl for whom he'd waited by the stage door.

# Chapter 15

'Jaysus, me heart just went crosswise, bounced off me liver, then scored a goal through me kidneys!'

*Seriously? Was just a little peace and quiet too much to ask for?* After trailing up and down towpaths, talking to any boat people willing to answer her questions and still coming up empty, all Julia wanted was to dip her toes in the sea of tranquillity. An hour or so, that's all she asked for, but any hopes of that were shattered the instant she saw the "Open" sign on her door and an Irish tornado turned the corner as she was digging her key out.

Orla wanted to plague Julia with questions? Fine. Julia was more than happy to freeze out this irritating reporter.

Except it wasn't Julia that Orla was talking to, was it?

'Did yer follow me here, Ben?' The blunt end of Orla's pencil jabbed a very expensive waistcoat between its top two buttons. 'Did yer?'

'Orla, please —' the young man said.

'Miss Keane to you, Benedict Tate. From now on, we're off first name terms. In fact, we're off all terms, full stop.'

'I've no idea how long you two intend to argue with each other.' Julia stepped between them, and only narrowly escaped being speared with a pencil. 'But you're not doing it on my doorstep. Inside. Both of you. Now.'

'No way! No way he's coming in,' Orla protested.

'Do you want to talk about scene of crime photos or not?'

'Fine, but if he —' Orla jerked her thumb — 'opens his gob, all bets are off.'

Julia closed the blind, and with a roll of her eyes turned the shop sign to "Closed." 'I think this calls for refreshments, don't you?' Either that, or a bucket of water over the pair of them. 'Orla?'

'Ach, the sun's over the yard arm somewhere on the planet. You got any o' that brandy stoff left?'

'I do.' Unless Mitzy and Minzi, Bitsy and Busy, or whatever their names were had filched it. 'What about you, Mr. Tate? What will you drink?'

'Call me Benedict.' He was even more handsome when he smiled. 'Ben. What I'd like more than anything is the blood of my enemies. Failing that, I'll have some of that brandy stoff, too.'

'Unusual hat,' Julia said, before Orla could sink her teeth in his jugular. Light in both colour and texture, it had a flat top with a black ribbon band. What set it apart were the two upturned side brims, bestowing a rakish appearance, which suited him down to the ground. 'Very stylish.'

'Thanks.'

His cheekbones were sharp, his blue eyes even sharper. They made a handsome couple, she thought. Dark and light. Fire and ice. Makes for a good combination.

'It's Parisian.'

'Parisian my arse! A gigolo's hat, that's what that is. The very sort you'd expect to find skulking after girls and waitin' to pounce.'

'You didn't mind me pouncing last night.'

'Last night was a one off, Benedict Tate. Yer'll not catch me in yer bed again, even if yer's the last man on earth.'

The right thing to do was for Julia to withdraw. Leave the lovers to slug it out. She refilled her glass and leaned on the counter.

'And there's me,' Ben was saying, 'under the impression that you weren't the kind of girl to indulge in one-night stands.'

'I'm not, and that wasn't a one-night stand, Benedict Tate, that was an interview, and for the record, you did not get the job. Now will you sling your boggin hook and let me get on with me work? This is the scoop of the century here, leastways for me, and you're ruinin' my chances with every second your shadow takes up space.'

'I've given you a story, Orla. That's a scoop, too. Why haven't you printed it yet?'

'Why? I'll tell you why. It's because I'm a journalist, and a good one, and I won't ruin my reputation with something that's rubbish, no matter how strong yer back is in bed.'

'Why do you keep saying that?' Ben was starting to thaw. 'Why won't you listen to me? Even if you don't believe it yourself, it makes for a damn good story.'

'It makes for libel, which means no newspaper'll touch it, and after that, they won't touch me, either.'

'Maybe if you investigated properly, you would see it's the truth.'

'Don't you dare question my abilities, Benedict Tate.' Stab, stab, stab went Orla's pencil. 'I've followed through till I'm blue in the face, can't yer just accept you're wrong?'

'Orla. I'm not wrong.'

'Miss Keane to you, and why can't you get it through your thick noodle? I'm not interested in a man who stalks me like I'm some kind of prey. I'm not interested in a man who won't admit when he's wrong. And I'm most certainly not interested in a man who thinks only of himself to the extent that he's prepared to wreck someone's career.'

'Wreck it? For God's sakes, woman, I'm trying to advance it. Why can't you get that in *your* thick noodle? They're simple questions, Orla, with a very simple answer. Why, when the window was broken, didn't he wake up? Why were only the most valuable items taken?'

'Darn and darnation, Ben, this is feedin' biscuits to a bear! I told yer. The police have a bloke in the clink for fencing the stuff. Now leave it alone, will yer, for your sanity and for mine, and let me crack on here.'

'Here.' He pulled a photograph from his wallet and showed it to Julia. 'My father.'

This was where you're supposed to say, my, my, you can see where you got your good looks from. Since it wasn't polite to suggest he must have inherited them from his mother, Julia waited for him to fill what was fast becoming an awkward silence.

'More accurately, my late father. My stepmother murdered him,' he said quietly, 'but Orla here refuses to accept it.'

The glass slipped through Julia's fingers, sending shards and cognac over the floor. As she reached down to pick up the pieces, she bumped heads with Ben, eager to help — but there was nothing amusing about a connection that would normally have broken the ice and put smiles on each other's faces.

Bentley-on-Thames. Posh town, posh houses, posh people. LOT of money lives there. For pity's sake, why hadn't Julia made the connection earlier?

'Please. Allow me.' Ben mopped up the cognac with what looked like a spanking new kerchief. 'You run a risk of cutting your hand.'

'Yours is armour plated?'

His eyes were kind. 'I'm not a photographer.'

Like shapes inside a kaleidoscope, the pieces didn't match. Julia ran through what Orla said earlier.

*There's this fella, see, convinced his stepmam killed his dad, and he's wrong. At least a hundred people saw the stepmam at the time the deadly deed was done, but here's what I mean about a story. There's this poor stook — well, when I say poor, I actually mean filthy stinking rich — found dead in his house, the place robbed to buggery, but the fella's son can't accept it's a simple burglary. Random acts of violence not figuring in his rarefied, entitled world. And with the servants also having cast iron alibis, he lashes out.*

Benedict's perception had been distorted by the lethal combination of shock and horror on top of the grief that comes with sudden death. Having lost his father — his only family — and with no one to comfort him and nowhere to turn, he blamed the only person left standing on the stage. The wicked stepmother.

Or not so wicked in this case.

And with random acts of violence 'not figuring in his rarefied, entitled world', he grabbed the nearest piece of flotsam in his storm-tossed seas and clung to it. That flotsam's name was Orla Keane.

Julia glanced at the girl, tapping her foot, her lips pursed almost white. These two had only just met. There was no disguising the electricity between them, but in the space of three days, he'd already taken the journalist to his bed. Was this an outlet for heartache? Or was he so broken by grief, that he was using her to influence her decision to print?

For a second, Julia saw herself in that scenario. She'd seduced Collingwood to pump him for information about the murders of her models, but that was a calculated decision, planned in advance. If you took a walk down the street — any street, anywhere in Britain — every woman you'd come across, from all ages and from all walks of life, would be scandalised by such degenerate behaviour. Nice girls don't, they would sneer. Nice girls wait until after they're married. Purity and restraint, they'd remind themselves smugly, were the lynchpin of the Empire. Rubbish. Lovemaking was one of life's greatest pleasures, and if it isn't, girls, find yourself another man.

Women would call her a strumpet. Men would call her a free spirit. Julia would call that perfectly normal. But Orla? Was she a free spirit? The familiarity between her and Ben stretched further than chemistry, but the question wasn't how far did it stretch. Rather, how deep.

Love at first sight was far from uncommon, and if Julia had to guess, she'd say Miss Keane had fallen, and fallen hard. And while Ben was obviously fond of her too, how quickly would those emotions readjust once he was thinking straight? Benedict Tate was fixated on hatred and resentment, tilting at all the wrong windmills, though in his defence, that's what sudden death does. In spite of everything, Ben was still Papa's little boy, inconsolable because there was no one in his life to console him. Julia understood why Orla was drawn to the tragedy.

Vulnerable but unable to show it, Ben might not even be aware that he was using the girl, but when the kaleidoscope twisted again, Julia saw another picture form in the same way she watched her negatives develop. The reporter couldn't see it. She was too close. But the ethereal creature at the heart of the drama wasn't Benedict Tate at all.

It was Orla. She was spirited. Smitten. Ambitious. Determined. But fast? Not this stormy Irish tornado, and though Orla would hate Julia for thinking it, the word that described her best when it came to Benedict Tate was vulnerable.

Like Ben, Julia had only known Orla a few days, but already she'd proved herself unexpectedly principled for a journalist, without compromising any sense of strong-mindedness, and not deterred in the slightest by obstacles strewn in her way. Most importantly, though, those principles oozed from every hot-headed pore, and if Ben Tate broke Orla's heart, so help her, Julia would cut out his liver, piece by little piece, and score goals with every sliver through his kidneys.

# Chapter 16

Three times Collingwood had been rendered numb, dumb, frozen to the spot in situations that no amount of police training could possibly have prepared him for.

The first time was three and a half years into the force, when he and several fellow peelers had been wetting the head of Constable Trigg's first baby in the Three Tuns public house on Meade Street. The entire group had taken off their arm bands, to signal that they were no longer on duty, which was just as well considering the vast quantities of ale sunk during the course of the evening. After the celebrations, the various parties went their different ways, but in a comparatively small jurisdiction, it was inevitable that several would take the same route before splintering off.

Had he and the new father not stopped on the corner to continue the banter with another officer before heading off together in the same direction, living, as they did, two streets apart, or perhaps if they'd dallied longer, the night would have turned out very differently. Instead, he and Jimmy Trigg linked arms across one another's shoulders, took two diagonal steps to the left, two diagonal steps to the right, then zigzagged up Cadogan Street singing vulgar words to popular songs, completely unconcerned about the life-threatening hangover that would await them in the morning.

They were into the second verse of the third song, or possibly the third verse of the second song — memories blur after a while, especially after that amount of beer — when they heard the rattle. In those days, of course, that's all policemen had to raise the alarm. A heavy oakwood ratchet, swung round by its handle. Eleven years ago, whistles superseded the rattle for a number of reasons, not least because they were lighter and less cumbersome, and couldn't be wrested from the officer and used as a weapon against him. The greatest advantage, though, was that their piercing shriek carried twice as far, meaning that when he and Jimmy heard the rattle, they knew the emergency was close.

The two sobered instantly, following the sound to a respectable terraced house where a domestic dispute was in full swing, lights blazing and the front door open to reveal a bull of a man in his shirt sleeves, with his fists bunched and his face red and twisted with anger. Cowering on her knees against the wall, hands over her head for protection, was a woman whose blouse was torn, and whose nose, face and neck streamed with blood. Between the pair, an embattled constable was doing his best to prevent further injuries by trying to push the husband back with one hand and reaching for his truncheon with the other. Strong as he was, his efforts were no match for fury and brute strength.

'Whore!' The husband swatted the policeman aside like he would a wasp. 'You dirty, filthy slut!' And just like any annoying wasp, when the policeman came between the two of them again, he laid him out with a single punch. 'Running round with other men —'

The slap sent her flying. 'Dan, please! I never —'

Collingwood and Trigg simultaneously reached for the handcuffs in their pockets. Without a word being said or a glance being exchanged, both knew that this would be a two-man job.

'Don't lie to me, bitch.'

A boot went in, and despite his father's criticism of the path he had taken, Collingwood was able to demonstrate that a good public school education wasn't wasted. Tackle low, lead with your shoulder, keep your head up — the perfect rugby tackle brought the aggressor down. Trigg grabbed his right wrist and manacled it firmly.

'Let's see how hard you can swing a punch now.' He grinned at Collingwood as he manacled the left. 'Because you, sir, are under arrest —'

'Oh no, you don't,' the woman screamed. 'You're not taking him away —' Trigg was still grinning when the frying pan shattered his temple. 'He's a good man, is my Dan —'

*Wham, whack, smack.* Blood everywhere. And brains. And bone.

That wasn't when Collingwood froze to the spot. In situations like this, instinct kicks in. He let go of his prisoner and lunged at the woman, who might well be a punching bag, but whose rage and resentment was without measure, clapping on the cuffs before she could inflict further damage. But the sad truth is that, ultimately, cast iron versus human skull is no contest. None at all.

And that was the first time Collingwood couldn't think. Or move. Or speak. It was a situation that no amount of police training prepares you for — seeing your friend's face obliterated beyond recognition. Knowing that an hour ago, he had everything to live for, but within another hour the young wife who had just given birth would learn that she was a widow, and his only child would grow up never knowing his father. All because he'd tried to help someone.

The senselessness, that's what Collingwood couldn't understand. For months afterwards, he'd experience flashbacks in excruciating detail, sweating to the point his shirt, sometimes his whole uniform, was drenched. He couldn't sleep. He'd find himself doing something completely ordinary, like eating breakfast, talking orders, pounding the beat as usual, when suddenly his heart would start racing, his muscles would tighten to iron, his breathing would become so hard that it hurt, and his stomach would go into spasm.

Coward that he was, he'd go to any lengths to avoid situations that might trigger the memories, but, of course, all things must pass. Naturally, the memory of that night remained with him, and the questions "could I have stopped it?", "what did I do wrong?" and "would I take the same course of action again?" still replayed in his head today. Funnily enough, one of the most surprising aspects of the whole affair was the lack of relief or liberation when he held Jim Trigg's widow's ice-cold hand while she watched the bitch who murdered her husband for no reason hang.

But life goes on. The rawness fades. He had a job to do, and part of that job involved promotion. Like most things in life, Collingwood applied himself with diligence and perception, gaining a reputation for attention to detail that quickly became his stock-in-trade. When he discovered that the ladder of police success bore rungs that pretty much compelled its officers to marry, that was fine, as well. He was hurtling towards thirty, and had sown enough wild oats to keep Scotland in porridge for a year. Disastrous though it turned out, marriage at least took his mind off Jimmy Trigg, and when Alice was born, the night terrors receded.

Alice was just one day shy of her fourth birthday when the second incident occurred — another moment where no amount of police training or experience prepares you for what happens next. It was broad daylight, this time, though once again, Collingwood was off duty, and being a detective sergeant by then, was in plain clothes. He remembered how happy he had been. In his pocket was Alice's birthday present — a delightful little glove with puppets for each finger. Kittens — how she loved them! Tabby, ginger, black and white, a different kitty for every digit, with astonishingly realistic faces right down to the whiskers, each dressed in a different miniature hat with matching miniature taffeta skirt that reached down to the second joint, so they danced every time the child wiggled its fingers.

When he'd turned the corner by the sugar refinery, he found himself face to face with a lascar in soft turban, maroon tunic, and white baggy cotton trousers swinging a yard of sabre-like curved blade. Later he'd learned that the sword was called a talwar, and the poor sod had been stranded five thousand miles from home, thanks to Government quotas that restricted the number of foreign sailors allowed to serve on any single ship. At the time, though, he had little interest in the plight of abandoned Indian seamen, but a great deal of sympathy for the woman and two children that he was threatening to behead.

Terrified beyond the point of screaming, and with the toddlers too young to understand, the woman knelt, eyes closed, shaking uncontrollably. Without the benefit of a translator, Collingwood had no way of knowing that the sailor was holding them hostage in exchange for a passage home to Assam. Even if he had, he certainly didn't have time to send a telegram to the East India Company and ask if they would kindly re-arrange their quota! What he understood, understood only too clearly, was that he'd walked in on a maniac intent on killing anyone who came close.

And, shame on him, he froze. Standing there, in the shadow of the towering refinery, he might have been a statue. In fact, the lascar could have taken all three of his hostages' heads off in a single swing, and Collingwood could not have moved.

The gibberish grew louder. Angrier. More frantic. Looking back, Collingwood suspected the man was probably telling him to go, to fetch someone who could sort this out, find him this improbable passage to Assam. But he couldn't. He was numb, dumb, frozen to the spot, and when the lascar lunged, sword whistling through the air, he confidently expected it to be the last sound he ever heard.

Stunned beyond belief that he was still alive and the lascar was still yelling, gesticulating, jumping up and down, Collingwood's brain had snapped into action. He sat down on the cobbles, crossed his legs, and patted the ground beside him in invitation. The lascar dropped to the ground opposite him, crossed his own legs and fell into a passionate dissertation (as he discovered later) about the injustice of being recruited from his homeland then abandoned. Apparently, this was not uncommon. The factories in Assam were producing more and more tea, which in turn required more and more ships, which of course required more and more hands. Leastways, until the Government's quotas and regulations kicked in, leaving hundreds of seamen stranded in Britain facing poverty and worse. With winter approaching, no work to be found on the Docks for a foreigner who couldn't speak the language, even less chance on the canals, and with little more than thin pyjamas to protect him, the lascar resorted to the most extreme of measures. With hindsight, Collingwood realised that the man never intended to hurt anyone. He was simply desperate.

'You're lucky that blade whistled,' the desk sergeant told him afterwards. 'Whistling means a bad swing, son. Swishing, now, aha, well that's another matter. If you'd heard his talwar swish, then that, lad, would have been the last sound you ever heard.'

Odd, the things you learn from situations like that. Though for the life of him, Collingwood never learned how a ten year prison sentence was the answer. But now, it had happened again. Collingwood was numb, dumb, more rigid than a sculpture cast out of bronze. Because no amount of police training, no amount of experience, ever prepares a man for facing the wife who murdered his only child in cold blood.

# Chapter 17

'Y'know, I never realised I was such a comic, till I started talkin' to meself.'

'Orla? I thought you and Ben left ages ago.'

'He left, and good boggin riddance. Me, I bin waiting for you to come back, and no, before yer wet yer knickers, I didn't pry, much as I was tempted.' Orla jumped off the counter where she'd been sitting, swinging her size four lace-up boots. 'Sold a china dog, though.'

*Please tell me it's that ugly bull mastiff.* 'Which one?'

Orla's pointy little nose wrinkled. 'Not sure what breed exactly. Some poodley thing...?'

*Oh, well.* Julia wouldn't have to look at the mastiff for much longer.

'Why d'yer sneak off, anyways? There was no need to give me and that lunatic privacy, because I'm not seeing him ever again, and that's a fact.'

'First of all, I didn't "sneak" anywhere, I had an appointment at the solicitor's, and secondly, it was only right that you two should make up in privacy.' Julia had retreated at the point where Orla had threatened to have Ben's cobblers for kebabs unless he started to talk sense.

'Make up? Are yer coddin' me? Seven billion nerves in me body, and he gets on every one of 'em. What in the name of the Apostles was I thinkin' of, getting involved with that man? I tell yer, he's depriving a village somewhere of its idiot, and that's a fact, too.'

'The more you protest...'

'I made a mistake and it hurts, I'll grant yer that —' Orla trailed Julia into the kitchen, where the scullery wasn't just still packed to the rafters, stocks seemed to be swelling. There was no sign of Mitzi and Minzi, for which Julia thanked God. Her eardrums had sustained enough assault for one morning. 'But I've learned me lesson. I'll make better mistakes termorrer, that much I promise. What were you doing at the solicitor's?'

'Benedict Tate is not a mistake.' Julia reached for a joint of roast beef marked from no. 12 on a card in flowery writing. 'His father was murdered, the house was ransacked, he's grieving, he's hurt and he's angry.'

'He's got to yer, hasn't he? I tell yer, that boy's blarney could talk the eyes out of yer head, and then sell 'em back to you for double the price. Can I snitch a piece of that game pie over there? Me stomach's rumbling worse than a train in a tunnel.'

With eyes that probably rolled out loud, Julia motioned the reporter to join her for lunch, and once again, she'd never seen so much food disappear so fast on a frame that put the average beanpole to shame.

'I watched the two of you,' Julia said, loading horseradish on to her beef. 'Before I was even aware of Ben's background, it was obvious there's a deep intimacy —'

'Me Mammy, rest her soul, would spin like a top, if she knew I'd given meself to a bloke who'd be out of his depth in a puddle —'

'I'm sorry about your mother, but I'm not talking about that kind of intimacy.' What Ben needed, Julia explained, was someone to sit with him, through the night if needs be, holding him, listening to his irrational ramblings without interruption or judgment, and basically letting him talk it out of his system. 'What he needs, Orla, is a friend.'

The shovelling stopped. 'Jaysus.' Orla laid down her fork. 'What a bitch yer must think me. What a bitch Ben there must think me!' She pushed the plate to one side. 'Hand on heart, the only thing I ever wanted was for him to face reality, 'cause that's me job, see. Record facts, report facts. And the facts is, fifty witnesses can — and indeed have — testified to seeing his stepmam at the time his dad was butchered. She was in the boggin high street, for crying out loud!'

'He tossed in the word gold-digger, as I recall.'

'Ach, she's a fine looking woman, I'll give him that. Where his old man, god love him, had a face like a blind cobbler's thumb.'

Julia recalled the photo Ben kept in his pocket and couldn't fault the description.

'So yeah, Blondie probably married Old Man Tate for his money, then again, mighta not. Stranger things have happened at sea. So I could've understood it, see, if he'd accused her of hiring some stooge to do the wicked deed on her behalf, but no. Ben's adamant his dad died by her own fair hand, and daft that I am, I was sure if I went through it enough times and showed him the proof, the daft sod would see logic and sense.'

'Which he will. Just in his own time, and in his own way.'

'Some friend I proved meself, eh?'

Julia gave an affectionate ruffle to the mass of black curls, as the tears spilled out of Orla's eyes. 'Nothing the word "sorry" can't put right.'

'You think so?'

'I know so.'

Orla blew her pointy little nose. 'Then that's what I'll do. Straight after me lunch, I'll go and apologise for making a boggin holy show of meself, and see if he's still willing to speak to me, again after I called him a horse's rear end and loads of other sweary words besides.' She pulled the plate back and speared a cold roast potato. 'An' if that don't work, I'll let him slip his hand up me skirt. Never fails. 'Cause don't forget, I've still got me piece to write. The one about grief twisting the most gentlest of souls. Now tell me again what it was yer was doing back there at the solicitor's.'

What Julia had been doing was handing over a document to be notarised — a list of all the furniture, linens, crockery, cutlery, etc. from this place to set the old ladies up when they were eventually rehomed, and extensive it was, too. After all, Jennifer James (Mrs.) would hardly be needing to sit on a blue velvet sofa while she captured Niagara Falls in its frozen, winter state. Sideboards are little use when you're trying to photograph the Sphinx. And when you're compiling books on Tombstone, Arizona, a place that had already gained a reputation for being the town too tough to die, bone china teapots do tend to get in the way.

In fact, Jennifer James (Mrs.) was only too happy that none of this stuff would end up devoured by moths or rot through with mould, and whether the old ducks preferred Willow Pattern to her pink and white Hammersley china, or her taste in paintings, rugs and curtains was diametrically opposite to theirs, was immaterial. There was enough furniture on the list to get them comfortable and started, an official document was needed to prove the sisters hadn't stolen them.

'Rewriting my will.' Julia stacked the plates with an innocent smile. 'The fire at the old ladies' makes you think, doesn't it? Anyway! To the important bit. Custard tart or trifle?'

Food was on Aaron's mind, too, or, more accurately, the lack of it. A solitary pickled herring was the only thing he'd eaten since last night, and funds were running low to non-existent.

He'd tried selling his tailoring trimmings, because even though he'd be a shilling down, a few coppers in his pocket was better than nothing. No one was interested. Understandably, they saw a tramp and decided that if he couldn't take care of himself, why would he take care of his trimmings?

He could always apply to the Jewish shelter, of course, but this was a fluid arrangement, where people from all walks of life who'd fallen on hard times threw themselves on its mercy. Suppose there was a poster on the wall? A Metropolitan Police Notice offering a £50 reward for information leading to the arrest of Aaron Adelman, wanted for murder? Time had passed — he looked older than his years, he'd changed his name and was used to fibbing about his background — but the basic description remained unchanged and if you looked closely at the picture, which they were bound to have, you'd recognise him without question. His path had crossed with dozens of clients, both during his sojourn on the road and in his capacity as a jeweller, but few of those, if any, would associate the assiduous little craftsman with murder if their eyes caught the poster. The Jewish community, on the other hand, was small, and far more likely to keep a look out for one of their own. What better incentive to help the poor than keep the poster in plain view?

£50 was an awfully big incentive.

Could he trust them, anyway? Every other day, Poppa would relate cautionary tales of Polish, Russian or Romanian Jews disembarking at St. Katherine's Dock and being scammed by their own countrymen. It started with telling the new arrivals that tickets for trains leaving the docks could only be purchased through a booking agent, and by the time various commissions and expenses had been deducted, the immigrants would be lucky to keep a quarter of the funds they arrived with. Add on the costs of board and lodgings, plus the fees for helping them find non-existent work, and most ended up on the street, sick and destitute, while the vultures feasted.

Stomach cramped with hunger, Aaron shuffled on in his two-sizes-too-large shoes, ignoring the blisters where they rubbed his bare feet. Finding work wouldn't be difficult, if he'd been prepared to change direction. The trouble was, deep down inside, he still nursed dreams of returning to his old life — sketching out designs, poring over trays of precious gems until he found the right stones for his piece, engaging in the intricate work of setting them. Never mind the pride in seeing a job well done, and imagining the fruits of his labours glittering round the baroness's neck at dinner, dangling from a duchess's ears at a charity ball, or glinting in the hair of a Prussian princess as she curtseyed to the queen! Not that his pieces went to such lofty clientele. Aaron was no fool, this was simply how he saw them in his mind's eye, both back then and now, and surely it would be a betrayal of his skills to take on heavy manual work and risk damaging his fingers?

The shipbuilding yards in the North East required massive labour forces, as did the new London docks, and there was always work aboard the steam ships, if he was desperate. There was even work in Oakbourne, loading and unloading on the railways or canals, if push came to shove, or portering for the railways. Trouble was, within a week, his delicate hands would be ruined, and there would be no going back after that. His days as a jeweller would be over forever — and without hope, what was there to live for?

He cleaned the glass on spectacles, taking special care with the cracked lens on the right. Clerking was an option. If he could somehow manage to smarten himself up, there might be vacancies for inexperienced men, though such posts normally went to women. The omnibuses were always on the lookout for drivers and conductors. Maybe he —

*Gigi?* He replaced his spectacles and blinked. It was her in the crowd!

Tripping over a Pekingese on a lead, he charged through the baskets and bags of the shoppers, mumbling 'sorry, sorry, sorry' with every lunge and elbow, but he was damned if he would lose her this time. *Oh yes. It was Gigi, all right.* No mistaking that swing of the hips in that flouncy lavender dress. The beautiful mountain of hair piled high beneath a bed of feathers that swished and swayed with every step. No woman in the world tipped her pretty head on one side like her! At the kerb, she paused to let the paraffin delivery cart clop by, and as she turned to check for obstacles, pedestrians and traffic, his breath caught in his throat. All these years! All this time and she hadn't changed a bit! Those big, blue eyes were as beautiful as ever. Skin smooth as alabaster, and oh, that little kiss curl on her forehead that no pin could discipline.

*Gigi, Gigi, my darling girl!*

She was approaching the new theatre. His hands were sweating, his breath ragged with exhilaration. He thought she was dead. He'd heard the last breath leave her body.

She wouldn't get away from him this time.

At the foot of the steps, she half-turned, smiling the same wide, warm, wholesome smile she wore when kicked up her shapely legs on the stage. The same wide, warm, wholesome smile she'd flashed at him in the front row. Except this time her smile was directed at the two men who hurried to join her. Tipping her head back with a laugh, she held both arms out sideways in a theatrical gesture. The taller, dark-haired man with the elegantly curled moustache and expensive brown tweed suit made a great show of linking her left arm with his.

The second, tubby round the middle but nonetheless stylish with his cane and high starched collar turned down in wings, took her other arm in equally melodramatic fashion. Together the three of them ran up the steps and disappeared inside the restaurant.

Two men. One tall, dark, and devilishly handsome. The other debonair and charming.

Aaron slammed his head against the pillar again and again and again.

# Chapter 18

A woman had been cut down in her prime, her body left to rot, and all Julia had achieved — all anyone had achieved — was bugger all. Sod arguing that this wasn't her fault, that solving crime was police work not hers, and she'd be on the train out of here the instant the line opened again, anyway. What mattered was, you can't get involved with the victims, then bugger off halfway through. You can't make promises to a dead girl, if you don't mean to keep them.

Rowena deserved a headstone. She deserved justice. She deserved to know someone cared. Right now, the only person who was gaining from this catastrophe was a killer, and the longer it went on, the slimmer the chances were of catching him. And what that bastard deserved was a noose.

Julia walked through the Common and waited for the coalman to clop past, sacks packed tight and upright in the cart — a reminder that these warm days and sweet nights were deceptive. Soon the colour of the leaves would turn to rich reds and bold amber, the air would grow chill, the nights would turn cold and the grass in the mornings would be tinged with frost. While the shire plodded its weary way, she glanced across at the window of her shop.

'Why didn't you have the glass engraved "Samuel Whitmore, Photographer?' she had asked Sam once. 'Why Whitmore Photographic?'

'Because it's different, JJ. Stands out from the competition.' Sam had run his hands through his Buffalo Bill hair to make his point. 'Smacks of our American cousins, don't you think? When people in fortunate circumstances have options, they tend to choose the most exotic. Too foreign and they're put off, don't ask me why.' He'd let out his gravelly chuckle. 'But evoke images of Paris, New York, Rome or Vienna, and you're home and dry.'

The shop blinds were down, the sign read "Closed", the old girls were obviously out, but when Julia unlocked the door, it was to find a detective inspector sprawled all over her chair, feet on the counter, crossed at the ankles.

Even in the semi-dark, Collingwood looked awful.

'Have you come to arrest me?' Julia asked.

'Is there a reason I should?'

She tried to pass it off as a joke. Made a quip about putting his handcuffs to better use upstairs. None of it came over remotely amusing.

'Are you busy?' he asked. 'There's something I'd like to discuss, only Charlie — Well. Good copper and all that, but...'

'You need a woman's perspective again.'

'No.' His mouth pursed. 'I need a friend.'

There was no longer a drawing room on the premises. Or a morning room. The business of photography had commandeered both, and the parlour was too formal, the kitchen too casual, the study had become a library of neatly boxed and catalogued plates. Without a word, Julia led Collingwood upstairs, closed the door and waited.

'I feel bad about loading this on to you —' He moved to the window and loosened his tie. 'It's Alice.'

*Oh God.* 'She died?'

'Worse.' He slumped on the bed and buried his head in his hands.

Sun, slanting in through the half-open window, showed up the layer of dust on the dressing table. Sparrows chirruped under the eaves. The band of the Salvation Army set up outside the draper's next door, telling shopkeepers and shoppers in music and song how they'd found a friend in Jesus and He was everything to them.

'This is my fault.' His voice was thick. 'Not that crap about being responsible for Alice's illness — for Christ's sake, how that was supposed to work, anyway? Criminal residue sticking to my clothes like some kind of, I don't know, invisible toffee — and what? Alice hugs me, then all this evil and blasphemy transfers to her? Or was it when she breathed in, that the sins from whatever villains I'd dealt with that day jumped off and miraculously made a home in her lungs? At the expense, I might add, of everyone else's? But it is my fault that my daughter died.'

When was the last time he slept, Julia wondered? When was the last time he smiled? When, dear God, would he be able to smile again?

'I should have clamped down on my wife's idiocy at the beginning,' Collingwood continued. 'Nipped the whole stupid thing in the bud, and told her once and for all that clothes don't trap sin, whatever the definition of that might be, and criminal tendencies don't transmute into tuberculosis, or the whole bloody world would be coughing its guts up.'

There was a time, Julia mused, not that long ago, when physicians believed long skirts trailed germs into the house from the street, and that consumption was either hereditary or the result of corsets restricting the circulation of blood from the heart. But though science in general, and medicine in particular, had advanced a long way since then, it was still fashionable for women to keep out of the sun, on the basis that pale isn't just beautiful, it's a sign of wealth and prosperity. Pale-faced women don't work in factories or on the barges or in the fields. Instead, pale-faced women dab bright spots of rouge on their cheeks, to make themselves appealing. What the hell was attractive about imitating TB?

'But no. Not me. Not John Know-it-all Collingwood. I thought it was my wife's way of coping with Alice wasting away, so I turned a deaf ear to her ramblings, and said nothing when she insisted that if I quit the police and gave my heart to God, my daughter would be cured. By the time I confronted her with the idiocy of her logic, she was beyond reasoning with, and again the fault lies with me.'

Keeping quiet was driving Julia mad. She should do something. Point out the idiocy of his own logic, too.

'I should never have married her, Julia. I was fond of her. Obviously. At the beginning. But I never loved her, and it wasn't fair to marry a girl on that basis.'

'Did she love you?'

'Honestly? I don't think she's capable of love. Not in the sense you and I see it, anyway.'

Once, Julia had asked Sam how you knew when you were in love. His answer was, *you'll know when you find it, JJ*, but she was young, then. Barely eighteen. *Is it when you'd die for someone?* she pressed, and would never forget his reply. *No, JJ, it is not.* She thought of her mother. Her brother. What she'd done for them. *Is it when you'd kill for that person?* she'd asked tremulously. Sam was well aware of her past. There were no secrets between them, and Sam didn't judge. *Not that either.* He'd given her cheek an affectionate pinch. *When you'd travel the universe and twist time for someone, JJ. That's when you know you're in love.*

Julia cleared her throat. 'Silly question, but why did you marry her?'

'Many reasons.' A snort of false laughter passed through Collingwood's lips. 'None of them honourable. It was after the riots. You remember the riots?'

She shook her head. They took place long before Sam set up in Oakbourne, in the days when photographic plates needed to be developed within ten minutes of taking them, and she and Sam were still on the road.

'It wasn't a patch on the London riots eight years ago. Ten thousand protesters, four hundred arrests, God knows how many injured. And it wasn't the Irish issue, either.' The ones he was referring to, Collingwood explained, came in the wake of a tragedy at the concert hall over in Southolt. 'It was the run-up to Christmas, the kids were excited, and when, I think it was Dixie the Clown, announced that the first fifty up to the stage would each receive a present, pandemonium broke out. The kids in the gallery rushed for the stairs, only to find someone had accidentally bolted the doors. As a result, ten children were crushed to death. The youngest was just three years old.

'There was outrage that a disaster like this could have happened and no one held accountable for their deaths, and once the national papers ran with the story, that was it. A crowd whipped up, and before you knew it, missiles were being hurled, windows were being broken, shops looted, fires started. Every police officer and reservist for miles around was drafted in, me included. The riots only broke up when the Grenadier Guards were called in. Seeing them lined up in their red jackets and big bearskin hats, bayonets fixed, was enough for even the staunchest protester.

'That was the limit for me, too. Watching normally law-abiding people turn into snarling rabid dogs, bludgeoning policemen and stabbing their horses, was the breaking point for my bachelor lifestyle. What better antidote to anarchy, bloodshed, thieving and murder than demure little Emily? Believe it or not, I found her devotion to pre-marital chastity quite enchanting, and as for being detached? I convinced myself this was an expression of iron self-control, and for my sins, admired her for it.'

His haunted grey eyes locked with Julia's.

'The irony, eh. I made my bed, and my wife refused to let me lie in it.'

'You made the wrong decision, and you both paid a price,' Julia said gently. 'But the price was a bad marriage, John. Not Alice's life.'

'I wish you could have met her, Julia. She was such a beautiful, bright little spirit. Happiness radiated off that child like rays from the sun, yet it wasn't her joy that was contagious in the end, it was that bloody White Plague. And because of me, her own father, she's dead.'

'This — listen to me — is not your fault.'

'Oh, but it is.' He disentangled himself and stood up. 'It is my fault, Julia. I knew Emily was sick. These rantings about God, and me bringing evil into the house, this business of not wanting a nurse, because Mama knows best. That's not normal...'

'You've suffered unimaginable loss and I can't begin to imagine the pain, but if you won't be kind to yourself, John, then I will.' She took both his hands in hers and squeezed. 'You worked and drank your way through Alice's illness. That was your way of coping. Your wife found other ways to see it through. She twisted logic to make sense of something that was otherwise senseless, but honestly? If that's what gave her strength to carry on, who's to say what's right and what's wrong?'

'What's wrong, Julia, is that it's my job, every father's job, to protect their child. I left Emily to her own devices, not because I felt it was best for her...' He pulled away. 'I let her carry on, because I thought it was harmless.'

The air in the room twisted.

'What do you mean?'

'Have you watched someone suffering from consumption? I don't recommend it.' He turned his body away from her, to the window. 'The hope. That's what got me. Watching her improve — dare I say blossom — crossing my fingers, feeling my heart leap, thinking this is it, she's finally turned the corner, only for the coughing and wheezing and vomiting to return, leaving her drenched in sweat and weaker than ever.'

The more he talked, the faster Julia's stomach churned. She could see the little girl's paper-thin skin, blue veins pushing through it. Heard the strain of a small stomach, bringing up blood. The rasp of ulcered lungs. Smelled the watery discharge she couldn't control. The clove-like scent of the laudanum Emily fed her to ease the pain.

'She died of a laudanum overdose?'

'That I could live with.' Collingwood lifted his face to the sky. 'That I could even be happy with, but what I didn't realise, and should have, because the signs were all there, under my nose, in my own bloody house, were the classic symptoms of arsenic poisoning.'

These warm summer days were deceptive, because the instant the sun dipped behind the trees, the temperature plummeted. Under the bridge, the same bridge where he'd found the dead man hanging and whose two-sizes-too-big shoes he was wearing, Aaron's teeth chattered. This was hardly surprising, given the wet state of his clothes and no means, and nowhere, to dry them off.

Once again, he'd had to wash them in the canal, only this time it wasn't a few splodges of meat and gravy from the pie. This was the blood from where he'd bashed his head against the pillar so many times he'd lost count, and blood, especially that much blood, wasn't such an easy stain to wash out. And the stupid part was, he hadn't even realised he was bleeding until somebody stopped him, and of course faces will spurt such copious amounts.

There were good people in this world, though. Despite the sorry state of him in his battered suit, saturated in blood, ditto his shirt and his hat, one kind Samaritan helped him into the barber's, then another, this time the barber himself, staunched the flow and patched him up.

'Don't tell me. Wait till I see the other bloke, eh?'

Aaron had been in no mood to joke. In fact, tears were streaming down his face, something else he hadn't noticed. 'I can't afford that,' he stuttered when the barber's apprentice handed him coffee and a hot sausage sandwich.

'Call it an early Christmas present, mate,' the boy had said. 'Me mum makes me far too much for me lunch anyway.'

Aaron's throat clogged at the kindness. 'Thanks, son.'

The boy was lying, of course. And there was no way of knowing he didn't celebrate Christmas, but even though, a mere hour earlier Aaron was starving, he had great trouble forcing the food down. With one eye swelling fast, Aaron had fished out his last remaining coins to pay for the medical attention.

'On the house,' the barber had said, rubbing on a pomade for good measure. 'I know grief when I see it, mate. That was just how my wife acted, when our boy fell under a train.' He scrubbed his eyes with the back of his hand. 'Only larking about on the platform with his brothers, then wham! He was gone.' He blew his nose. 'So put your money away, and promise me you won't get into any more fights with inanimate objects?'

Good men were few and far between. How Aaron wished he was one of them.

Shivering, he looked around. The canal people were tucked up in bed for the night, curtains drawn, boats in darkness, ready for an early start in the morning.

He had been a good man, once upon a time. Back in the days when he designed floral pendants and dazzling tiaras — and dragonfly brooches he gave to certain girls in the chorus.

Hand on heart, all he intended was to follow Gigi today, when he spotted her in the street. Find out where she lived. Smarten himself up even if he had to beg, borrow or steal, and call on her. Tell her he was sorry. So, so sorry. Tell her the truth. That, in his heart, she had never died, then say 'Can I buy you dinner?' as though he was standing at the stage door.

But when he saw her, linking arms with those two men, he knew none of that was going to happen.

He strained his ears in the darkness. There was no sound, other than the plop of a rat in the water.

The sky was changing colour. Soon it would be light. Soon they would find the body at his feet.

# Chapter 19

Having developed the last of the prints from the crime scene, Julia carried the pile to her studio and set them out as though she was back at the site. Some she laid on the floor, some she propped upright, others she pinned to the wall with drawing pins, or else to her props to create a three-dimensional view.

What time Collingwood left, she didn't know. He'd talked about Alice, her giggles, her dancing, her hugs, the games they played together, the walks they went on, the pet rabbit he bought her, the toy theatre they built together, the kitten finger puppets he'd picked up for her fourth birthday. Which led him to talk about the lascar, the swishing sword, the taking of hostages, and his diffusing of the situation. Which led him to talk about situations no police officer — no father — can be prepared for. Facing the woman who murdered your daughter. And just when Julia thought his throat was too sore to speak, he talked about the rage that welled up. How it took every ounce of self-control to keep away from the house where Emily was being held, for fear of what he might do.

'Christ, Julia. Is there a worse betrayal of trust than a desperately ill child believing her mother is making her well?'

He hadn't wanted to eat, but she forced him to anyway. Even grief and despair need fuel. Downstairs, she'd heard the old girls fussing about, doing their laundry, making dinner, washing up, but when a soul is in torment, worrying about what the neighbours might make of a young widow entertaining a married man in her bedroom was irrelevant. For one thing, it was far from the entertainment most people imagined, and for another, the target of this insidious gossip would be long gone by the time word got round. So, as St. Oswald's chimed their lives away, Collingwood had talked, he cried, he eventually slept. Then Julia fell asleep. And when she woke up, he was gone.

Not a word. Not a note.

She wasn't surprised. He'd come here wanting a friend. She had listened. But when you split your soul open, exposing every vulnerable inch, laying bare every weakness and failing, the relationship changes. She doubted she'd ever see him again. And maybe there was a silver lining here, too. With the whole town under the impression that scandal had driven her out, wouldn't that would buy her even more time?

'Here you go, dear. Nice big breakfast.'

Engrossed in laying out the photos, Julia hadn't heard the old ladies come in.

'Set you up for the day, this.'

'We didn't bring eggs.'

'We knew you were busy.'

'And you wouldn't be able to eat them in your lovely studio.'

'Too messy.'

'We didn't cook kippers, either.'

'Too stinky.'

'So we brought toast, with orange marmalade from Her at Number 5.'

'And some ham.'

'And a big pot of coffee. Shall I pour?'

*Dear God. It was like keeping budgerigars.* The thing to remember, Julia kept telling herself, was the old girls meant well, even if their twittering did make her want to jump off the nearest ledge with a heavy weight strapped to her ankles.

'Oh, Lord, is that the poor girl from behind the old theatre?' Mitzi/Betsy crossed herself.

'Died sometime on Monday the *Chronicle* said.' Minzie/Bitsy ran a wrinkly hand over the photos. 'Left like rubbish until that tramp stumbled over her poor body on Tuesday morning.'

'She'd still be there now, if it wasn't for him.'

'I didn't mean for you to see them,' Julia said.

'Oh, don't worry about us, dear.'

'Saw worse than that in the Crimea.'

'Far worse.' The younger one shook her head. 'Amputations, gangrene, blindness, madness, whole shoulders shot away, burns, disembowelment, that's only the tip of the iceberg.'

'You were nurses?'

'Scutari. That's where the sick and wounded were sent, you see.'

'We'd been caring for patients at the gentlewomen's hospital in Cavendish Square when Miss Nightingale was appointed superintendent. When War broke out and she was asked to go to Turkey, we volunteered to go with her.'

'But oh, my! Our poor boys! Four thousand died that first winter, you know, and only one in six from their wounds.'

'That battle hospital was a disgrace!' The older sister's eyes narrowed in pain. 'Filthy, overcrowded, no blankets, no decent food. Dreadful.'

'We were supposed to be fighting the Russians.' Thin lips pursed tighter. 'Instead it turned out cholera, typhus and dysentery were the enemy.'

'Under Miss Nightingale's directions, we set up a kitchen, fed the men from our own supplies, cleaned them up and, more importantly, kept them clean, while Florence arranged for the sewers to be flushed and ventilation to be improved.'

'Death rates fell dramatically, and Hattie and I are proud to have played a part in that.'

'Very proud.'

*Hattie.* Not Mitzi or Betsy or Izzy. The woman's name was Henrietta. Hattie. Shame rippled down Julia's spine. How easy it had been to make fun of these two. Dismiss them as foolish old ducks, every bit as shallow as she'd considered them one-dimensional. How horribly, horribly arrogant. 'Is that where you met? At the hospital in London?'

'Yes, we were —' The younger one pulled up short. 'Oh.' The silence was awkward, but it didn't last long. 'How long have you known?'

'That you weren't sisters?' Should Julia tell them she'd had her suspicions all along, but it was actually the one master bedroom, the one double bed, all their clothes in the same room, that gave it away? 'A while.'

They exchanged glances. 'But we look so alike.'

'No. You dress alike. You mimic each other. You eat the same things to retain the same weight.' Or lack of it. They were as skinny as ferrets. The whole thing was an act. 'You set out to make people believe what their eyes tell them, same as this echo business, and finishing each other's sentences. And forgive me for saying so, but you also make yourselves deliberately annoying, to ensure people leave you in peace.'

'You did!' The younger one giggled. 'Dived into a hedge in Cadogan Street once.'

'Guilty as charged.' Julia's cheeks were burning that they'd not just noticed, but that it was seared in their memory.

'Two old spinsters, daft as duck down? No one questions it, dear, and you know what they say. Ask me no questions and I'll tell you no lies.'

'Listen, sweetheart, we need to let Julia get on with her work.' The younger one poured coffee that was barely steaming while Hattie buttered slices of toast that had gone cold. 'This is important work that she's doing. Not just pioneering a new investigative technique, but helping this poor lady, who can't help herself.'

'Reminds you of how you helped the soldiers in the Crimea?' Julia asked.

'We like to think we made a difference, yes. And that's what you're doing here. Making a difference. We won't keep you.'

Alone again, Julia returned to the prints, except she wasn't looking at Rowena this time, and refused to be drawn into the pathos of patched underclothes, the callous way her body had been left, and the indignity of being left for the rodents. This exercise was about examining the scene as a whole, and this time with complete objectivity.

She'd always told herself that, if she ever took up a job as police photographer, she'd take dozens of pictures, as opposed to the handful the Parisian police took. What was the point in doing half a job, especially with the advances in film-on-a-roll in box cameras? Surely it made sense to capture every angle, every spurt of blood, every item dropped at the scene, or damaged or broken, recording for ever what had been disturbed and what had not? An overturned chair, for instance, smacks of struggle or rage. The room where nothing is out of place hangs a killer in the snap of a finger, once the jury are shown images of a planned and cold-blooded attack.

She nibbled on the soggy toast.

*You've given us a first rate female perspective on this case.*

Maybe, she thought, licking marmalade off her fingers before joining two of the photos together. But an artist's perspective? That's a different dimension. No doubt like her, the Parisian photographers ran their own studios and took portraits to pay the bills, any police work that came their way simply a sideline. But from what she'd seen of their compositions, they were more clinical analysts than artists.

Cold coffee was forgotten as Julia reached for the magnifying glass. Rubble, by its nature, is irregular, and time softens jagged contours with weeds, debris and moss. But here. She squinted. Here, rocks and stones had been pillaged from the side, leaving the pile lopsided and clean. Since the object of the photographs was to record the victim and conserve the crime scene, the surrounding area hadn't received a great deal of attention. Police constables had searched the derelict theatre and the waste ground round the body, but no one had thought to expand the search area. An oversight she would have taken great pleasure teasing a certain detective inspector about, had the circumstances been different.

She scanned the glass across another section of prints until she found what she was looking for. There! Right next to the buddleia that kept attacking her during the course of her crime scene duties. *No moss.*

Her heart beat that little bit faster. No moss on this pile of rubble. No weeds growing out of these stones. Not so much as a daisy. Coincidence?

She unpinned the print from the wall and the shop bell tinged.

'Top o' the mornin' to yer, me darlin',' trilled Orla in a comically exaggerated accent. 'But enough about me. Grab yer camera, they've — Jaysus Mary Magdalene, is this all your work?'

'Orla! I thought we'd agreed —'

'I forgot, I forgot, cross me heart and hope to slip on a banana skin, it went straight out of me moind, but this! Holy shamrocks and barmbrack, this is amazin' work!'

Julia couldn't decide whether to hug her or smack her. But Orla was right. Crime scene photography was going to change the course of criminal investigations in the future.

'Yer a boggin genius, that's what you are.'

'And you —' With her black curls and black eyes, Orla was striking to start with. Add on a white cotton skirt with vertical black stripes and matching jacket trimmed with black lace and piping, and the effect ramped up to stunning. Top it with a broad-rimmed hat in the same fabric embellished with a giant black bow, giant as in bigger than the reporter's whole head, and — 'You're going to be responsible for a veritable orgy of street accidents, you know that, don't you? Can we can safely say that things went well with Ben, then?'

'That it did. He's coming round. Slowly. I think.'

'He has no one else to blame for his father's murder.' Julia tried not to think of the Collingwood tragedy. The analogies were too close. 'But —' she pasted on a smile — 'I'm guessing you didn't come here to show off your fancy new outfit.'

'Oh, I wore it to show off an' that's a fact. Ben bought it for me yesterday, said I looked as pretty as a picture. But what I came for was for you to grab yer boggin camera. Now get a move on, will yer! They found a body beside the canal. Bloodbath, I heard, so grab yer coat. We gotta get in quick.'

Julia's scalp prickled. 'Sorry, Orla. Only Detective Inspector Collingwood has the authority to —'

'Murder don't stop just 'cause one lazy sod took the day off.' Orla's black eyes rolled. 'These bosses, eh? Think 'cause it's Saturday they can bugger off when they feel like it, swanning around like a king doing nothing and saddling me with Charlie Cod of all people. Ach, will yer hurry, woman! I need me scoop!'

'The plates are too heavy for just you and me.' The canal was hardly round the corner.

'Just as well reinforcements are to hand, then.' Orla opened the shop door and stuck two fingers in her mouth. The whistle could have pierced steel. 'My Ben's big and muscly, aren't yer, lad?'

*Poor Ben*, Julia thought, loading him with glass plates. Did he know what he was letting himself in for with this Irish tornado?

Julia could have ducked out, of course — easy enough, given that Boot Street hadn't sanctioned her involvement. But another murder, when Collingwood still hadn't told his superiors about the killing that took place inside his own house, was the last thing he needed, and besides, Julia needed to draw Sgt. Kincaid's attention to the rubble behind the theatre. Two birds with one moss-free stone.

To her shame, Julia's first reaction when she reached the canal was relief. All the way from her studio, she'd expected to find another Rowena, head bashed in, stripped of her outer clothes, then dumped (as the old girls put it) like rubbish. In fact, she'd already given the new victim a name. Hermione. Why a man's body, lying twisted, disfigured and abandoned, should be better was hard to explain.

'Well, well, if it isn't the lovely Mrs. McAllister.' Charlie Kincaid tipped his camel bowler with a rugged smile. 'I don't know whether to shake your hand or duck.'

'A wise man would duck.'

At that moment, three mallards flew over the canal, quacking like crazy. Bloodbath or not, they both sniggered.

'No sign of his watch, chain or wallet, sarge.' The uniformed constable shone his bulls-eye lamp on the victim. 'Robbery without a shadow, I'm afraid.'

Kincaid turned to Julia with a twinkling smile. 'How about you, Mrs. McAllister? Any shadows of doubt in your mind?' This wasn't robbery, they both knew it.

'The attack was personal,' she said, more to herself than the sergeant. 'The fact that his face has been beaten until every feature's been obliterated shows anger. Someone hated this man very much.'

'Didn't they.' Kincaid's gravelly voice rumbled through the tunnel. 'He even took his shoes to prevent us tracing the victim. Right then.' He gave his hands a brisk rub. 'I'll move my men out of here, give you space to take photos.'

'Ah, well, we have a problem there, Sergeant.'

When Orla said a body had been found, what she didn't say — probably didn't know — was that the body was under a bridge. Without artificial help, it was too dark to photograph a thing down there, assuming there was anything left to record. Most of the morning traffic had passed without a second glance at the drunk passed out on the tow path. Tramps often camped out under the bridges. One more inert body hadn't stood out. It wasn't until a boy guiding a horse-drawn barge stumbled over what he thought was a man who'd had an accidental fall that the alarm was finally raised, by which time it was too late to prevent evidence from being lost. The entire scene was a mass of footprints from everyone who'd rushed to help. The outline of more than one horseshoe stood out in the congealed blood. More than one person had spewed at the sight.

'Perhaps when you bring the victim into the open, I can record his injuries. Even then, there's little that wouldn't be better photographed, once he's been cleaned up in the morgue.'

'Would that be the murder weapon, then?' an Irish voice piped up. 'That sticky red lump?'

'Get her out of here,' Kincaid growled at the constable.

Didn't he realise that pushing her back, out of the tunnel, supposedly out of the way, only fed Orla's enthusiasm?

'Is she right?' Julia asked.

'Unfortunately, yes.' He scowled down the tunnel. 'Tentative blow to start with.'

She understood. The skin on the scalp was particularly thick, and, being fed by an extensive blood supply, meant superficial injuries bled profusely. Or, as he put it —

'Like a geyser.' After which, Kincaid said, rage took over. 'I'd hate to say how many times that rock came down on his face.' He scratched his chin. 'The good doctor will obviously need to confirm the cause of death, but my guess is that our snappy dresser here died from blood loss.'

Julia's stomach flipped. Was that the case with Rowena? Was she alive while she was being pushed and pulled and dragged and stripped? Aware of what was happening, but too weak to stop it? Had she died, fully aware of the humiliation that she'd be facing?

Julia looked down at the loud checked suit. The arm hanging over the bank. The manicured hand trailing in the canal, inches from the constant procession of painted hulls chugging past.

'Aha!' Kincaid took the lamp from the constable and shone it directly on the tailor's label inside the dead man's jacket. 'Killer's not quite as clever as he thought. He took the shoes to prevent identification, but either he's unfamiliar with quality tailoring, or he forgot, or he panicked. We can trace this suit, and therefore the owner, no question.' He handed the lamp back. 'Bloody sight quicker, if someone reports him missing, of course.'

With no photographs to take, there was no point in Julia hanging around. At the top of the embankment, Ben was standing guard over her camera, along with her tripod and plates, having his ear bent by an Irish firecracker venting her frustration at not being given an interview by the police in general, and Charlie Boggin Cod in particular.

'Come on, Julia, you'll tell me, won't yer. Who is the man they're dragging out now? Where's he from? Is that sticky red lump really what killed the poor stook?'

Julia shrugged. 'Sorry, Orla.'

'Oh, please! Gimme something! You've seen the fish eye Charlie Cod keeps on giving me. He hates me, that man.'

Julia was about to explain there was nothing she could add when Ben cut in. 'Sergeant Kincaid's a policeman. He hates all journalists, darling, so instead of hanging around crime scenes where you won't get an answer, why don't you write about who killed my father?'

'Me job's to report the news, Benedict Tate, not to make it.'

'But —'

'But nothing.' Orla wrinkled her nose. 'Look, I didn't mention it earlier, I knew what you'd say, but the peelers recovered a few more of your father's possessions this morning. His pocket watch was among the haul, and that's gotta be a comfort, hasn't it? Having his —'

'Any sign of my mother's jewellery?'

'It'll turn up eventually.'

'No, it won't. The bitch took it. I told you. The watch was no use, so she dumped it, along with any other pieces she couldn't dispose of, knowing someone would find it, pawn it, get caught and, if she was lucky, hang for murder. If not, it still takes the heat off.'

'Bennn —!' Orla's dark eyes rolled in Julia's direction. 'Your stepmam doesn't need to do any of that. She can claim on the insurance.'

'Except this way, she gets the money twice and, thanks entirely to you, she's getting away with my father's murder, as well.'

'You can't seriously think I'm submitting an editorial of the basis of a light sleeper not waking when the downstairs window broke?'

'She killed him, Orla. She was a gold-digger from the outset —'

'A gold-digger who was seen by five hundred people. Now for the love of God, can't we please dance to a different tune, Ben? For instance, did yer mean it, when you said yer'd buy me supper at the Café de Paris?'

'I always keep my promises, Orla.'

'Then promise not to talk about this anymore, or it'll put me right off me trotters and tripe.'

Julia picked up her camera and as many of the glass plates as she could carry and left Orla and Ben to it. She ducked past a man carrying a bundle of thatch on his shoulders, side-stepped two boys rolling a hoop and smiled at a toothless vagrant smoking a broken clay pipe, then turned back.

'Funny. I could have sworn you'd left.' With a wicked grin, Kincaid pointedly pulled his hat brim down.

'I'm a woman, we have a knack of being in two places at once, and don't worry, Sergeant. I have no intention of denting my tripod with your head.' She put down the stand, camera and plates and dug out the prints she'd almost forgotten.

His mood instantly became serious. 'What am I looking at?'

'These two piles of rubble.' Julia's hands were shaking with excitement. 'This one is fresh. This is where the stones were taken from.'

'You think that's where —'

'The clothes are buried? Yes.'

*Find the hat. Find the owner.*

One step closer to putting a name on a headstone. One step closer to justice.

# Chapter 20

'Thank you for agreeing to see me on a Saturday.'

'Not at all, Inspector.'

Collingwood had forgotten just how young Dr. Harrington's lanky build, fair hair and downy moustache made him look.

'I fully understand why you wouldn't want me to call on you at Boot Street instead.' Harrington held open the door to his surgery and motioned him to take the seat beside his desk. 'Coffee?'

'Thank you.'

The doctor's house was halfway down the hill, towards the station. One of a long line of impressive residences built in the late 1850s to accommodate businessmen and professionals, perhaps the sort of house Collingwood would have lived in, had he succumbed to pressure from his father and trained as a physician. Double frontage, welcoming red brick, acre gardens, so far from its neighbour you'd need a megaphone to chat. Another reason why the Old Man had been so snotty about his son's choice of profession. Had he been able to afford this kind of neighbourhood on police pay, his father could happily have ignored the shameful occupation he had chosen, and cheerfully overlooked the unskilled, low-paid, working-class backgrounds of his fellow officers who clearly wouldn't mind sleeping four to a room and sharing table and dresser in a wreck of a building in which there was no sanitation.

Oddly enough, it wasn't Collingwood's first choice of accommodation either, but you don't sign up for the job if you can't put up with a few inconveniences and are worried about what people think. Even those closest to you. You sign up because you think you can make a difference. *Think* being the operative word.

Collingwood's father used to have a surgery such like Harrington's. His smelled more of disinfectant and cigars than the musky amber cologne worn by the young doctor and, perhaps it was memory playing tricks, but the examination chair, as he recalled, was decidedly less comfortable. The Old Man was dead now. In a corner of the cemetery these past fourteen years. Idly, Collingwood wondered whether, if he'd lived, he'd have attended his wedding, come to Alice's christening, been here for his granddaughter's funeral. The answer to all three was the same.

'I assume you have the analyst's results?' Collingwood asked.

'I do. They were delivered yesterday morning. As it happens, the results make interesting reading.'

'For a father, a husband, or a policeman?'

'All three.' The young doctor cleared his throat. 'As you know, I performed a basic test in my surgery by passing hydrogen sulphide through the specimens taken from your daughter. From this, I was able to detect the presence of arsenic. Simple but effective, and, given the child's symptoms, enough to justify an expert opinion.' He leaned across and laid a hand gently on Collingwood's arm. 'I believe you said you were familiar with the Reinsch test?'

Collingwood nodded and, in a bid to distance himself from what was coming, scanned the tomes of medical books locked away behind glass in a gleaming mahogany bookcase. It didn't stop his stomach from knotting.

'Dissolve body tissue in hydrochloric acid,' Collingwood said. *His baby girl's body tissue...* 'Insert copper strip. A silvery coating indicates mercury poisoning. A dark grey metallic coating could be anything from arsenic to antimony to selenium poison.'

'Correct, although the laboratory obviously took a more detailed scientific approach, placing a copper plate that had previously been treated with nitric acid in an arsenic solution that in itself been acidified with hydrochloric acid and heated almost to boiling point.'

'That merely rules out mercury.'

'Ah. Well, combined with the yellow precipitation I sent across to the lab, I'm afraid it rules out everything except arsenic. I won't bore you with the pros of halide ions being present versus the cons of chlorate ions, but remember this test was devised long before you or I were born. As you'll know from your own line of work, Inspector, the Marsh test is a far better way to demonstrate the presence of arsenic.'

'Isn't that test equally old?'

'It is, just as it is equally definitive, as I'm sure you're well aware.'

Harrington looked wet behind the ears, Collingwood thought, but appearances can be deceptive. No medical practitioner would make a better witness on the stand. Especially when he's testifying for the Prosecution...

'If, by processing the samples,' Harrington was explaining, 'arsine gas is found to be present, this can be oxidised to leave a deposit of arsenic on the glass.'

'The so-called arsenic mirror.'

'Exactly. This allows the depth of colour to be compared to deposits produced earlier using calibrated amounts.' Harrington leaned back in his swivel chair and steepled his fingers. 'The measurements are exceptionally precise, Inspector.'

'Robert Peel,' Collingwood said slowly, 'ruled that every police officer should be issued with a warrant number that would identify him personally, to ensure that each officer was accountable for his actions.'

'You are not accountable for your wife's actions.'

'Except this happened inside my own home, Doctor, which means every case, every single case in which I have been involved and there are thousands, will be scrutinised. Every single person I have sent to prison will appeal.' That Collingwood would lose his job went without saying. Kincaid, too, since he was implicit in what would be seen as a cover-up in not reporting murder. The Top Brass would take this as the very excuse they needed to close Boot Street station.

'Not necessarily.' Harrington wagged a confident finger. 'The fact that your wife fooled Dr. Poulson shows how easily she was able to manipulate the situation.'

'Hm.' Pacing the room, Collingwood's eyes alighted on the leather bag, buckled in readiness for an emergency call. Inside, among other things, was the doctor's stethoscope, thermometer, tongue depressor, reflex tester and syringes, along with bandages and the likes of tincture of iodine, morphine, digitalis and cough syrup. How many times had Alice had one of those bags laid on her bed? Far too many for one short, little life. He stopped pacing. 'Robert Peel also advocated that trust and transparency were paramount to the force, and that every officer should exercise integrity in the power entrusted to him.'

'The Hippocratic Oath is not dissimilar, Inspector. Do no harm.'

'Good.' Collingwood cracked his knuckles. Right from the wee small hours after he'd left Julia's, his mind had been whirling, churning, processing, assessing, weighing up what next. 'I was hoping you'd come round to my way of thinking.'

# Chapter 21

Autumn would soon be nudging summer aside, carrying the tang of ploughed soil and wild mushrooms on the air. A rolling spectrum of colour and mood, peppered with the *chack-chack-chack* of the fieldfare in the hedgerows, the dusty scent of haystacks towering in the fields, and jewel-bright starbursts of winter daffodils.

Standing by the bridge this morning, Julia had been keenly aware of the two faces of Oakbourne. The leafy, respectable half, with its butchers, bakers and candlestick makers, winding medieval lanes and pretty Saxon church, around which elegant suburbs were springing up like weeds. Contrasted to the other half, with its glowering factories and deafening mills that clogged the lungs of their workers and drove them to paupers' graves ahead of their time.

On this side, big hats, big feathers, big sleeves, all silks and satins and dainty heeled shoes, twirling parasols to keep delicate faces from burning. On the other side, they'd be lucky to catch a glimpse of the sun. Men, women and children in tatters and rags would be lined up at the gates, begging for work or huddled under the arches begging for food. No carefully barbered whiskers for them. No crisp creases in their trouser legs. No expensive fragrances to splash on their pulse points. Most would be grateful for a bowl of fresh water to wash in, and far too many were forced to sleep in dormitories eight to a room, where the beds were so close, the fleas strolled rather than jumped.

But whether top-to-toe lavender or reeking of bloaters and gin, in rustling silks or rough clothes, invigorated by afternoon tea or exhausted after their shift at the gas works, what they had was routine. As familiar for everyone on both sides of Oakbourne as night followed day followed night.

What Julia would not give for that. To be a normal person, going about their normal business...

Factory workers might be covered in soot, forced to stretch every last farthing, and solicitors might be vexed by finding piano teachers for their daughters and hiring reliable servants, but the one thing they had in common was that they all had friends. They had family. They had children and husbands, and large or small, their houses would ring with laughter that Julia had long forgotten. She didn't even have the luxury of her father in his coffin. His features, may he rest in peace, had long since been overridden by time, and the memories of chasing her kitten round the kitchen, sneaking raisins from the jar, the sweet kiss of her mother as she tucked her up in bed had blown away like smoke in the night.

Her stepfather saw to that.

These days, when Julia thought of being tucked up at night, it was the cold knot of fear at his steps in the hall. It was her mother who was chased, cowering at every blow the bastard delivered, trying not to cry out lest the children should hear. There were no raisins to sneak, because there were no treats in the house. Just Julia and her brother, clinging to each other, hands over their ears. Whispering to themselves, to block out the sound.

Now, thanks to her, the Devil was dead, and she had no regrets about killing him, because, may they rot in hell, the police refused to help. Whether by kinship or marriage, they were Trevellicks to a man, and they made their stance abundantly clear. What happened inside a house was the homeowner's business. There was no case to answer when it came to assault.

Some lesson, eh? Seven years old, and she'd already learned that, sooner or later, everyone lets you down.

Another seven years passed before the suffering became unbearable, consigning her to a life that left her isolated from the rest of the world, with the knowledge that she would never have a family to come home to or kiss her own child goodnight. She daren't even strike up a friendship, not a deep one, and as for keeping kittens, forget it. Like death and taxes, one other thing was for sure, at some point, she'd be on the move and another identity would have to kick in. Julia couldn't afford emotional attachments.

Look what happened when she got close to her models...

All the same, twirling her parasol to shield her delicate face, it was impossible not to be swept up in the joy of the Indian summer, which brought out the town's typical eccentricities. The small boy with trousers hitched comically high in his braces washing the windows of the Welsh dairy. The blind man with the massive handlebar moustache playing Schubert's Serenade on the violin with tear-jerking perfection. Mr. Lund, the chemist, all veined cheeks, red nose and heavy scowl, blocking his own doorway as he rocked on his heels, and wondering why everyone flocked to Evans's down the road for their camphors, shaving foams, and balsam of Peru for their piles.

Not forgetting the taxidermist's on the corner, which, like the Museum of Anatomy, remained a perpetual draw, though not necessarily for educational purpose. Sometimes he'd showcase squirrels in dinner jackets, playing cards and smoking cigars round a table. Other times he'd have a two-headed calf on display, or a dog playing croquet. Once, he filled the entire bay window with a full-sized gorilla — at least that's what he claimed it to be. Julia was no expert, but to her it looked like a baboon.

Eventually, she arrived at the graceful Georgian building that housed the offices of Griffin Insurance, where she found Harold Turrow.

'Mrs — uh — uh —' he stuttered.

'McAllister,' she confirmed with the very warmest of smiles. 'Thank you for seeing me without an appointment.'

'Not at all, not at all.' He had to raise his voice over the clack of typewriters, stencils and addressing machines. 'Saturday's our busiest day. Need to keep on top of things, y'know. Follow me.' A pudgy hand beckoned towards an office partitioned off in the corner. The name on the glass door read *H.J. Turrow, Branch Manager*. 'I presume you're here with the signed disclaimers?'

Julia had forgotten about the skin that was too white for its own good, highlighting freckles that were an unfortunate consequence of gingery hair. She had almost forgotten his nasal whine, too. What she hadn't forgotten was Harold Turrow's superior manner — as ugly as the green tiled floor.

'Not exactly.'

'Ah. You wish to take out a policy of your own. Very wise.'

'I thought we might negotiate terms for the damage.'

'My dear Mrs. McAllister.' Could a smile be more condescending? 'I understand how difficult it must be for the proprietors, and I'm sure the ladies appreciate your support and intervention, but my hands are tied.'

'Mr. Turrow, you deliberately left Griffin's fire plaque on the outside of the French sisters' house as a form of free advertising.'

'We covered this point in your parlour.' The whine became more pronounced as he grew impatient. 'Perhaps *the ladies* —' he stressed the word to include Julia — 'in the misery of their misfortune, have forgotten. Insurance companies no longer have their own fire brigades.'

The very reason the plaques were made of iron was to withstand the heat of the fire and identify which insurer should be notified. The companies' priority was saving property, rather than lives. Their goal was financial, pure and simple.

'Even when municipal brigades were introduced,' Julia said, 'they were pressured to favour houses covered by insurance against those that weren't.'

'Quite irrelevant, Mrs. McAllister, quite irrelevant. The crux of the matter is that the purpose behind installing fire plaques is long out of date.'

'Yet you didn't remove it.'

'Technically, I was not obliged —'

'Technically, nothing.' Julia pulled out the original documents and laid them on the desk. 'The agent who sold the ladies this policy, and by agent I mean you, knew exactly how much they could afford, and that if fire was included, Griffin's premiums were beyond their means and they would look for cheaper insurance elsewhere.'

'I —'

'You were also under pressure to make this sale, because you wanted promotion, and promotion, correct me if I'm wrong, is based purely on the number of contracts signed.'

'I didn't force them into anything.'

'No. You misled them, which is worse. Unfortunately, unlike force, it is not punishable by law, but you will make this right.'

'Are you mad? You want me to forge a backdated contract?'

'Good grief, no. You'll be no use to the old dears in prison.' Julia leaned forward and laced her hands on the desk. 'What I want you to do, Mr. Turrow, is make an ex gratia payment to cover the structural work. You know, the floorboards, the ceilings, the plumbing, the roof.'

'You're an embarrassment to yourself, Mrs. McAllister. I will have to ask you to leave.'

'Please don't. I'm enjoying myself far too much. Anyway, the question isn't whether you should be asking me to leave, but how large is the cheque you're going to write.'

'This is ridiculous. I'm calling the doorman.'

'Why is it ridiculous? You used your fire plaque as an advertisement. All I'm suggesting is that it pays for itself. Once word gets round that Griffin honours its commitments, you'll acquire an awful lot of clients on the back of it. The company will be seen as a benchmark for integrity, stock prices will soar, you'll be promoted to a bigger office, while two harmless old ladies will have a roof over their heads, which they certainly won't, if you stick to your current line.'

He leaned back and looped his thumbs in his waistcoat pockets. 'For a woman, you make a sound argument, I'll give you that. Unfortunately, you can't flatter me into changing the rules, Mrs. McAllister, and you certainly can't badger me into it, either. I know you feel sorry for them, but the fire was their own fault. By their own admission, they left a candle burning where the curtain could catch it, and as for their belief that our plaque covered them, as I stated before, ignorance is no excuse. They should have read the fine print on the policy.'

'Oh, dear. I can't appeal to your better nature, I can't kindle your commercial instincts, and flattery isn't working.' Julia sighed. 'It would appear that I'm right out of options.'

'That you are. Tell the ladies I'll expect the signed waiver on my desk first thing Monday morning.'

'No, no, you misread me, Mr. Turrow. I said it would *appear* I'm out of options. I didn't say that I *am*.'

'If you're thinking of blackmailing me by implying the terrible things the *Chronicle* will write, should you take the story to them, believe me, I've heard it before.' He smiled a cold smile. 'Do your worst.'

'I intend to.'

She laid another envelope on his desk, and his skin turned even whiter. Because it had finally dawned on her where she'd seen Turrow before. When her investigations had taken her deeper into the saucy picture trade than she'd ever intended, or indeed wanted, to go, she'd interviewed a photographer who specialised in homoerotic postcards. The sort that could send a man to prison.

'This ... photograph... Where did you get it?'

'Which photograph, Mr. Turrow? The one where you and six other men are cavorting like Romans at an orgy, or the one where you're tied to the bedpost while Mr. Whiplash does what he's best at? Or the one where the Headmaster, at least I think he's a headmaster, since the only thing he's wearing is a mortarboard, has you over his knee and is spanking your naughty, white, naked bottom.'

'I...' Turrow reached for the chequebook with a shaking hand. 'I presume I can count on your discretion?'

'I promise. You will never hear or see me again.' Julia smiled. 'Nice tassel, by the way.'

# Chapter 22

Julia felt a corner had been turned, and believe it or not, she was glad Orla had made her miss the train. Now she could leave with some measure of peace in her heart, and not just on Harold Turrow's account. If she was right, and the victim's clothes were indeed under that fresh pile of rubble, it explained why the killer hadn't been seen carrying armfuls of bloodied silks and feathers through busy streets on Monday morning. Trace the hat, trace the owner — take a huge leap towards tracing the bastard who took Rowena's life then left her to rot in anonymity. Julia had played a part in delivering that justice, and it felt good. Better than that, it felt right.

There was satisfaction on a professional level, as well. Only by dispensing with the clinical approach of the Parisian police and taking numerous shots from various angles (including the harrowing one of the victim's last view before she died), had the anomaly been thrown up. Tactics Collingwood could now employ with his new crime scene photographer. And if Griffin Insurance and the hangman's noose wasn't enough to wrap a warm glow round her heart, there was, of course, the old ladies.

'You can't give us all this furniture, you won't have a stick left!'

'No, no, dear, we can't take your lovely sideboard!'

'You've put your dining table on the list. What on earth will you use?'

'You can't manage without chairs, dear.'

'Or the sofa.'

'That walnut dressing table, isn't that from your bedroom? I'm sorry, but we wouldn't dream of taking it.'

It took a while — not to mention patience she didn't know that she had — but eventually Julia convinced them that her Aunt Josephine had died and left her all her furniture, so the old dears would be doing her a favour by taking away her current things.

'I don't believe your aunt bequeathed you every piece of her china.'

'No one leaves their niece casserole dishes and saucepans, dear.'

'Or glassware.'

'Or cutlery.'

'By the way, I bumped into Mr. Turrow on my way back from the solicitor's,' Julia told them.

'The Man From The Insurance? What did he want?'

'More blood from a stone?'

'Funnily enough, he was on his way here, and since he was pressed for another appointment, I offered to save him the journey.' Julia passed them the cheque. 'The papers will be ready for signature first thing Monday morning. Meanwhile, he thought you might want to contact workmen regarding repairs.'

Many squeals, tears, hugs and the inevitable glass of celebratory Scotch later, the old girls were pinning on hats and buttoning their shoes to pay a call on a builder who came highly recommended, and see if he was available to start work right away.

Alone at last, Julia felt the house sigh with relief, but the silence brought no comfort.

Why is euphoria is so fleeting, when heartache's unending? Why should she feel guilty about being happy? Once again, she toyed with the idea of sending her mother and brother money. An anonymous gift, which couldn't be traced, especially since she'd emptied her secret bank account around the time her models were being killed. The moment, to be exact, that Detective Inspector Collingwood put her at the top of his suspect list and discovered her name was neither Julia nor McAllister, that she'd never married much less been widowed, and that everything about her was a lie. What stopped her was Sam, she could still hear his voice, warning her about her stepfather's family.

*You know what they're like, JJ. With him out of the picture the family will have taken over his role as controllers.*

Sam was right. Julia's mother and brother would never see a penny of what she sent. Instead, they'd be bullied all the more because of it. Her eyes stung for her mother, for her brother, for Sam. With him, at least, she'd been able to say goodbye. She'd laid her final white rose on his grave only last week. She still missed him, though, every damned day, this man with the Buffalo Bill hair and Buffalo Bill beard who rescued her, gave her confidence, gave her friendship, taught her photography, taught her peace, and brought unconditional love without judgment. The father she never had became the mentor whose advice she still lived by, and whose wisdom she could never repay.

*Sam, Sam, we had such good times, didn't we? Remember when we went to London for the Queen's Jubilee? We followed the procession to Westminster Abbey, cheered her as she stood on the balcony, then lost track of time and missed the last train back to Oakbourne! To console ourselves, we scoffed Denby pies by the bucketload. Remember them, Sam? Created specially for the Jubilee, they were dubbed Resurrection Pies because they were left for a week before being baked for a second time —*

'Hello...? Mrs. McAllister...?' There was no mistaking the gravelly voice calling out from the street. 'Anyone home?'

Julia wiped her eyes. 'Sergeant Kincaid.'

'Twice in one day, Miss — I know what you're thinking.'

'What a lucky chap you are?' Dusk had fallen, she noticed. The street lamps were lit, and the first chill in the air wafted through as she unlocked the door and let him in. 'Coffee? Tea? Cognac?'

'Tempting, but I can't stop. I dropped by to tell you that you were right. Our boys uncovered that weedless heap of yours, and sure enough, that's where he dumped — what did you call the victim?'

'Rowena.'

'Well, that's where he put her clothes and covered them over. Everything's there, least as far as we can tell. Hat — heavily bloodstained inside, I might add.' He read aloud from his notes. 'Lavender silk afternoon dress, matching jacket, parasol, shoes, gloves, silk petticoats.' He flipped the book shut. 'Right down to her white beaded reticule.'

Julia felt her heart beating faster. 'Anything inside which can identify her?'

'Well, there was a purse. But it's just a standard kiss-clasp with a few coins rattling around. Two threepenny bits, three ha'pennies and a farthing, if I remember correctly. A lace hankie, no embroidered initials, unfortunately. Oh, and a door key, though where that fits is anyone's guess.' Then he shot her his trademark wink, and she realised that he'd been stringing her along all the time.

'What?' she asked breathlessly. 'Enough with the suspense, what else did you find?'

'Suppose I said a ticket for a passage from Liverpool to New York leaving on Tuesday?'

'You're kidding!'

'Nope.' His craggy cheeks creviced even further. 'Your Rowena's name is Mary Mason.'

Julia's heart leapt. *Mary Mason! Her name is Mary Mason, and now she'll have a headstone where her family can visit. Her dignity will be restored. God willing, justice won't be far behind.*

'Someone didn't want this poor woman to leave.' Kincaid had pulled a face. 'Pound to a penny, Mary was escaping from a violent husband or an obsessively jealous gentleman caller. Being desperate for a better life, and as part of her new start, I wouldn't mind betting that she'd treated herself to a set of fashionable new clothes, either. Seen it many times,' he'd added. 'New life, new identity. Who's going to question it?'

*You mean apart from a detective inspector, with the grey eyes of a wolf and the determination and tracking skills to match?* 'Who indeed, Sergeant.'

'Sad to say, I know scum like this only too well. Doesn't matter which side of the tracks they live, woman are getting treatment for bruises, breaks and burns every bleedin' day, and the daft part? They point blank refuse to press charges. Some of the men belong in the if-I-can't-have-you-no-one-else-will box. Others are more the I'll-tell-you-when-you-can-leave type. Both are downright dangerous, because they keep pushing out the boundaries, changing the rules as they go along, and if you ask me, that's why he stripped off her fancy posh clothes then buried them. To take her down a peg, because that way, if anyone found her, this was just another nameless victim in cheap, darned underwear. Under his thumb in death, same as the poor cow was in life. Quite literally rubbing her nose in the dirt.'

As theories go, it was plausible.

After Kincaid left, Julia laid the prints on the table and examined them once again. First the victim, then the crime scene. There was something wrong, though where she'd seen Turrow but couldn't quite put her finger on it...

Footsteps sounded and the scent of Hammam bouquet wafted in with Collingwood. That clever blend of Turkish rose, musk and heart-stoppingly expensive orris designed to invoke images of naked bodies writhing in steam-filled tiled baths, of harems, dusky skin, and transparent gauze. His eyes were still set in deep purple pits, and his jaw remained tight, testifying to the most terrible turmoil a man would ever have to live through. But his backbone was straight, his chin was high, and that's what Julia admired and feared about DI John Collingwood. The death of his child at the hands of his wife had brought him to his knees, but it didn't break or destroy him. On the contrary, he'd mastered it, and that's why she needed to leave as quickly as possible. He already knew she was living a lie, just as he knew no one takes on a new identity without good reason. And if you don't confide to the man whose bed and body you've shared, the conclusion is that you have something unlawful to hide.

It was only a matter of time before he uncovered the truth. Time that was not on her side any more, now that Mary Mason's killer was this close to capture.

He pulled out the chair opposite and sat down. 'The shop door was open. I locked it behind me.'

The door was open, because in Julia's rush to work out what was niggling away, she'd forgotten to lock it behind Sgt. Kincaid. A serious and stupid oversight, given the money and passport just a few feet away. She wouldn't make that mistake twice.

'Coffee?' she asked.

'Something stronger?'

Julia filled two crystal brandy balloons, and set out a plate of oatcakes and cheese.

'No double act this evening?' he asked, looking round.

'Repair work starts on their house first thing Monday morning. The old girls are now worried how they'll cope with it all, so to take their minds off it, they've gone to the Music Hall.'

'Nothing cures the brain of worry quite like a night of bawdy songs and corny jokes.' Collingwood warmed the glass in his hands. 'Unless, of course, it's a bullet.'

Urbane, witty, but ever the professional. The quicker Julia McAllister became Jennifer James, the better.

'Charlie been round?' he said, leaning back and looping one lazy arm over the chair. 'Told you about finding the hat and the clothes?'

'And the steamer to New York on Tuesday.'

'See? Female perspective and a sharp artist's eye.' He raised the glass in a toast. 'Thanks to you, the net's closing in ... and yet.' Julia lifted a slow, quizzical eyebrow. He wasn't the only one who could keep emotions under control. 'Here you are. Poring over the crime scene. Again.'

'Your sergeant's probably right about Mary Mason's killer, only —' She sipped at the cognac, swapped the pictures around, and what do you know? The missing piece clicked into place. *Some of them belong in the if-I-can't-have-you-no-one-else-will box. Others were more the I'll-tell-you-when-you-can-leave type.* 'Kincaid's wrong. No self-respecting bully is going to attack her from behind. He needs to dominate. Right to the bitter end, he'll want to show this bitch who's boss.' Her stepfather taught Julia that little lesson.

'Christ.' Collingwood spiked his hands through his hair. 'Now you point it out, it's pretty damned obvious. Maybe you should take Charlie's place.'

'Not sure I'm cut out for snuggling up to a glass of porter and Mrs. Kincaid.'

'Who is?' He almost chuckled. 'Unfortunately, at the moment, neither is he, because you won't believe this — Boot Street has a crime wave on its hands.' He emptied his glass in one swallow and refilled it. 'A fourth murder in as many days.'

'I'm afraid that, without proper lighting, photos of the crime scene are next to impossible.'

'That's all right, the body's already in the morgue.'

'The pathologist's been murdered?'

The tension in his face relaxed. 'If only life was that simple.' He reached for the Wensleydale. 'Like our victim with the missing shoes, the scene was well and truly compromised by the time we came along, but I'd appreciate it if you could call round in the morning, after the victim's been cleaned up. His wallet's missing, but a photo should help identify him.'

'Of course.' The London train didn't leave until the afternoon.

'You know, the poor sod's still warm, and the *Chronicle*'s already decided on the motive and stirring up a hornet's nest out there.' He attacked the Stilton as if it was a journalist. 'Have you seen the paper?' He dug the front page of the evening edition of the out of his pocket. 'Talk about alarmist.'

Julia took it from him and read.

*The police are refusing to comment, but it's this newspaper's belief that both the latest victim and the body found this morning were targets for robberies. Both were rich swells, and we suspect they were butchered by a maniac with a grudge against men doing well for themselves, hating them to the point where they want to obliterate them.*

That wasn't enough to rile a detective inspector to the point where crumbly Cheshire cheeses feared for their life, though. Julia kept reading, and sure enough, at the end —

*Demonstrating yet a further slide in police standards, in which crime prevention no longer seems to take priority, the* Chronicle *finds that it falls on us to make the public alert to the current situation. We therefore beg each and every reader to be vigilant, and most importantly, be prepared to defend yourselves at all times.*

'Can you believe it?' His fist smashed down on the table so hard, the plates jumped. 'The paper's telling people to go out armed. How bloody irresponsible is that?'

Julia swirled the cognac around in her glass. His daughter was dead. His wife was responsible. Was any betrayal greater than that? Powerless, angry and bereft, he'd immersed himself in work to block out the pain, and he'd be inhuman if he didn't need an outlet for that rage. So it was pointless trying to reason with him. Tell him this is what newspapers do, because more than anyone, he knew how the press stirred things up. Better to switch the focus.

'Were the second victim's shoes missing?'

She noticed a few more grey hairs at Collingwood's temple when he shook his head.

'Only his pocket watch and what I suspect was a very fat wallet, because, as the *Chronicle* took great pains to point out, his tailoring didn't come from any slop shop, and his shirt was top-quality made-to-measure.'

'They're right, though. Oakbourne is suffering a spate of robberies by someone with a resentment, if not deep hatred, of wealth.'

'And I'll hate myself for saying this, but with luck, it's someone from the canals. Transient I can handle. Boot Street's stock-in-trade. Arsenic, on the other hand —' He pushed the plate away. 'Thanks to an exhaustive multiplicity of test-tubes, funnels, copper foils, tripods, Bunsen burners and other scientific gear and tackle, the laboratory has now confirmed what we already knew. My baby was riddled with this particular metalloid, and, when confronted with what is now irrefutable evidence, my wife confessed to feeding it to her.' The air turned cold. 'It was not her intention to kill Alice. She swears that on every word of the Bible, so it must be true, eh?'

Suddenly he was no longer the upstanding officer in charge of a police station. He was a bereaved father, adrift in a storm with no life boat. When Julia touched his hand, he jumped like he'd been stung.

'At first, I thought she was deluding herself. She prepared the damned food, for Christ's sake. What did she think was going to happen? But no. Right when I thought this nightmare couldn't get worse, my dear wife tells me she didn't mean for the dose to be fatal, she just wanted Alice to stay ill. Can you imagine anything more heinous,' he growled, 'than a mother torturing her child purely so she could gain the attention of the doctors, her husband, the congregation at her church? Deliberately and maliciously manipulating everyone in her sphere, including her desperately sick daughter, for her own aggrandisement? Which left me with something of a conundrum, to put it mildly.'

The hand that topped up the cognac was shaking. The hand that laid the empty glass back on the table was not. Exactly how much steel was in this man's body?

'The office of the Coroner was established back in the Middle Ages to investigate sudden, unnatural or unexplained deaths.' He could have been addressing a group of schoolchildren. 'Our modern police force goes back a mere blink in comparison, with their primary role — my primary role — to prevent crime, but then, once it's committed, build a cast iron case to bring the criminals to justice.'

How long could he go without sleep, Julia wondered? How long could he keep this up?

'The challenge I faced was how to reconcile these noble concepts without compromising the blindfolded lady who stands outside the Old Bailey.' He paused, and the lines round his eyes hardened. 'Until I realised how decent a chap Dr. Harrington is underneath that sickeningly youthful exterior.'

He'd called on Dr. Harrington this morning, Collingwood explained, proposing the doctor list a different cause of death on Alice's death certificate, one that would obviate any need for the Coroner's intervention.

Julia was numb. 'John! What in God's name did you tell him to do?'

'Well, for one thing, God has nothing to do with. That's Emily's department, not mine. And for another, Harrington is very much his own man. I couldn't pressure him into breathing, if he didn't want to.

'Imagine what the *Chronicle* would have made of a policeman allowing a crime like that in his own home?' Collingwood shrugged. 'Not to mention every newspaper up and down the country, casting suspicion on everyone in law enforcement from night-watchmen right the way up to Chief Constable in every force throughout the country.

'And how could I hide the manner of Alice's death from my superiors? Unless I play this right, the scandal will end up at the Home Office, probably on the Home Secretary's desk, given that every case I have investigated would be called into question, and every conviction I've been involved with would have doubt cast upon it. Potentially hundreds of villains could get a free pardon.'

'That —' Julia cleared her throat. 'That's quite a weight to carry.'

'Precisely why I needed to ditch it.'

'You're not seriously suggesting a cover-up?'

'Categorically not.'

Julia would have preferred a little more sincerity in his voice, but maybe that was because the room was spinning and she couldn't think or hear straight.

'Dr. Harrington and I discussed the issue at more than considerable length and we both agree that, despite the test results, the case wouldn't necessarily hold up in court. The defence would argue, rightly so, that the effects of arsenic are variable and uncertain, and that while Emily admitted administering the poison, it was not of a sufficient dose to conclude that she deliberately set out to kill her young daughter. On the contrary. They would argue that she mistakenly believed arsenic would help Alice get getter, in much the same way it's used to treat psoriasis and syphilis, and has been known, in certain cases, to improve the coats of horses and — this is the crucial bit — make them plump. The sympathy of the jury would undoubtedly lie with the mother.'

'To what then —' Julia was almost afraid to ask — 'did the doctor attribute cause of death?'

'Laudanum overdose, due to a heartbroken, overworked mother not realising how weak the tuberculosis had rendered her child, and inadvertently administering too great a dose of painkiller to a body that was simply unable to take it.'

This didn't make sense to Julia. *Do no harm* — that was the oath every doctor takes. 'How in God's name can Harrington live with himself, knowing that a murderer will walk free?' *How can you, John?*

'He can testify, under oath if needs be, how arsenic was present in Alice's body. He just couldn't swear it was sufficient to kill her, which is not a lie and tallies with Emily's account. But as for walking away, she won't. You don't put a child through sustained torture, kill her, accidentally or otherwise, and get away with it. Harrington signed a second certificate, certifying that Emily Jane Collingwood should be admitted to an asylum for the criminally insane, and remain there for the rest of her life.'

Collingwood knew he couldn't allow Boot Street to close. His priority was the jurisdiction his station served, namely keeping the people of Oakbourne as safe as he could. The Top Brass argued that a merger would result in better subdivision of labour and therefore better policing. Collingwood counter-argued that Boot Street might be stretched to capacity with just sixteen constables, Charlie Kincaid and himself, but the team knew these streets and their residents like the backs of their hand. This station was the equivalent of a small, cottage hospital, and he was damned if he'd abandon Oakbourne to a bunch of self-serving brown-nosers.

The paradox was that, because Boot Street was such a small intimate station, news travelled fast, and bad news meant rumours. Rumours which the penny press get to hear.

Newspapers, as everyone knows are, gospel, and before you can blink, fiction becomes fact.

Two years ago, a farmer in the Cotswolds died of arsenic poisoning, and a month later, his father dropped dead in the field. There was no evidence of foul play. The wife was a treasure, everyone said so, they worked well together, argued no more than any other married couple, had four fine sons between the ages of eight and fifteen, hadn't taken out an insurance policy, and there was no other man. The Coroner ruled that death was accidental ingestion of rat poison in the barn combined with the sheep dip he'd been handling, while the father was known to have a weak heart. It didn't stop the farmer's wife being branded a black widow, and when another man died in a nearby village, the gutter press picked up the story, embellished it out of all recognition, and the next thing you know, the area was named as a hotbed of poisoners where men and women flocked from all over the country, seeking advice on how to murder their spouses.

It was bollocks, the lot of it. Accidental ingestion of arsenic was pretty common, especially in the countryside, although, to be fair, fatal doses were rare. But with the likes of Mary Ann Cotton, disposing of her mother, three husbands, a fiancé, and God knows how many of her fifteen children and stepchildren purely for the insurance, ditto William Palmer, the notorious Prince of Poisoners, still talked about today as much as ever, you can see how easy it was to believe the twaddle in the papers. If word got out that an inspector's wife murdered her daughter, rumours would run wild. All manner of tripe would be bandied about — starting with how he and Emily worked as a team, eliminating anyone who got in their way, to killing for profit via vigilante justice. Collingwood wasn't prepared to stand by and let hysteria rule, purely to line editors' pockets. For that reason alone, Emily should never stand trial.

'An institution is the right solution,' Dr. Harrington had assured him. 'She may have known what she was doing, but she's still a sick woman.'

Collingwood wouldn't bet his life on it, but equally he couldn't risk her being found innocent. Chances were, she'd end up killing another trusting creature — and get away with that, as well. Committing her was the only answer. The trouble was, she'd either be sent off to Broadmoor or the special ward in Bedlam.

How the hell could he keep track of her there?

# Chapter 23

'Appreciate you coming, Miss.' Charlie Kincaid's cadaverous form seemed right at home in the hospital mortuary. 'Unfortunately, we won't be needing your services after all.'

'How come?' Julia was confused. She left the shop pretty much the instant he telephoned to say, quote, *the stiff was cleaned up and looking forward to having his photograph taken.* That couldn't have been more than half an hour ago, tops.

'Ah, well, a Mrs. Pike read the piece in the *Chronicle*, and when her husband didn't come home last night, she started to worry. Funnily enough, she was in the process of reporting him missing to the desk sergeant while I was on the blower to you.' Kincaid indicated the door to the left. 'She identified the remains as that of one Alfred Pike, but now you're here, it mightn't such a bad idea if you took a picture of the first stiff from yesterday. Not much to work with by way of facial recognition, but from time to time we get lucky, and who knows? Someone might recognise ... well, something about him.'

'Never take a job as a salesman, Sergeant.'

A gravelly chuckle rumbled round the white painted brick walls, which confined a coldness that went deeper, far deeper, than the temperature needed to preserve a corpse. 'I'll leave you to it, then, while I take a statement from the widow. The superintendent will show you the body.' His nose wrinkled as he indicated the small room off to the left. 'Couldn't question the poor woman here. Not with all these sinks, saws and tubes and stuff, and when it's her old man on the slab.'

Expecting the superintendent to be some dour individual looking like he should have retired ten years ago, Julia was surprised to find him to be short, bald, with a chin-curtain beard and tiny, twinkling green eyes. While he tucked up Mr. Pike, then proceeded to roll the cover away from yesterday's "stiff", she set up her camera and tried not to think about Alice Collingwood under the sheet on the adjacent table.

Committing women to institutions for killing their children was depressingly routine. Deemed "not of sound mind or capable of pleading", they could be committed at any stage during the judicial proceedings, from the time of trial right through to sentencing and imprisonment, but there were exceptions. Agnes Rouke, for one. At seventeen years old, she gave birth to an unwanted, illegitimate baby and claimed dogs had run off with it. Unfortunately, what Agnes gained in the creativity department, she lost when it came to cold, hard facts. The poor mite was found in the next door neighbour's garden, and a post mortem showed the infant died from being thrown from an upstairs window. A board of doctors and psychiatrists unanimously agreed that no sane person could have perpetrated such a wicked act. Off she went to an asylum for the criminally insane.

Then there was Margaret Blair, an equally young and impoverished spinster, who tried to give her new-born away, but, when there were no takers, left it beside the canal knowing one of the bargees would take pity and adopt it. Once again, a post mortem refuted the account. The baby died from drowning, the result of having had a weight tied to its little feet and dropped in the canal, an act which was attributed to the "mental disorders of pregnancy and childbed".

Not only did these cases not go to trial, the girls were considered mad, rather than bad, and as such would attract sympathy from both inmates and staff.

Julia couldn't help wondering how much sympathy Emily Collingwood would garner. Bugger all would be her guess. Harrington might well swing mad-not-bad to the Board responsible for signing the committal papers, but once inside those walls, it wouldn't take long for her true colours to show, and when they did, they would shine like sunlight on water.

Emily Collingwood was a magician. All these years, her husband had felt guilty about inveigling a naïve creature into marriage for no better reason than he was ambitious, under pressure from his superiors, and felt Emily would "make a good wife," and when he admitted his motives for marriage were less than noble, he wasn't bloody kidding. Unfortunately, we all have lapses of judgment, it's just that some demand heavier payment than others. John Collingwood had carried the burden like the Ancient Mariner's albatross — without any inkling that he was, in fact, the trick.

Emily Collingwood might have exploited her husband's weak spots and pulled the wool over the family doctor's eyes, but she wouldn't be able to fool the people running the asylum, any more than she would win over her fellow inmates. There would be no diagnosis of "weak minded" here. They'd soon see the woman was bad, not mad, and far from acting out of desperation, knew what she was doing.

'Here we go, all set.' Julia was jerked back to the reason she was in this icy cold place by the cheery voice of the superintendent, beckoning her. 'Now be a good boy,' he said to the corpse on the table. 'Smile for the nice lady photographer.'

'Do your charges often talk back?' she asked. Anything to take her mind off the lifeless bumps under the sheets as she lined up her shot.

'Better bloody well not.' He let out a laugh. 'I get enough of that from the wife.'

'Herb —?' A woman with tight blonde curls wedged under a mountain of ostrich feathers stood in the doorway, her white gloved hand to her mouth. Even in shock, she was gorgeous. 'No, no, no, not you, too!' Wide-eyed, she ran to the table. 'Oh, Herbie, love! Not you!' She turned tortured eyes on the superintendent. 'First my husband, now my brother...'

Wrapping her arms round Dora Pike's shoulders, Julia spun her away from the mangled mess on the table. They say lightning doesn't strike twice, but it does. Ask any mother who lost all her sons in different battles, or the man who lost one leg from disease then the other from a fall, neither of them his fault.

'Sit down.' Julia virtually pushed the woman into the chair in the side room where Kincaid had been interviewing her only a few minutes earlier, and Dora Pike would have sat, thinking life couldn't get any worse. 'Deep breaths, that's the ticket.'

'Their faces,' Dora said dully. 'Did you see what those monsters did to their faces? There's nothing left of my Alfie or Herb! Nothing!'

Julia knelt down beside her and took both hands in hers. 'Picture them as you remember them best. Keep that image in your memory. Not this.' Behind her back, she signalled for the superintendent to fetch Sgt. Kincaid.

'I didn't think twice when Herbie didn't come home.' The woman's blank eyes fixed at a chart on the wall, blissfully unaware that it was a gruesome anatomical diagram. 'Fast women and slow horses, that was my brother.' She smiled. 'I used to tease him about that something rotten, I did, and it was on account of them little fancies of his that he'd be gone for days at a time. Not Alf, though. Not Alfie.' She turned to Julia. 'You married?'

This wasn't the time to maintain any pretence of widowhood. 'No.'

'Most of us freelance professionals in the sisterhood aren't, but me, I got a ring on my finger soon as I could.'

'How did you and Alf meet?' Anything to keep the conversation going. Julia daren't let the poor woman fall apart now.

'I were a Tiller Girl in Manchester, me, but ooh, that Mr. Tiller. What a tartar. Moan, moan, moan. On and on about lack of discipline in the chorus line, so he had us link arms so we'd all dance as one.' She tossed her lovely blonde head. 'Well, I weren't having none of that. I'm an artiste, love. No one bosses me around.'

'So you left Manchester?'

'In a manner of speaking.' Dora glanced round to make sure no one was listening. 'Bugger sacked me, and I quote, for being "wilful, wayward and drunk".'

'Were you?'

Dora giggled. 'Bet your sweet arse! Anyroad, that's when I met the Pike boys. Cousins, both quite a bit older than me, but ... well, you know what it's like.'

'Every girl likes a man with a past.'

'True enough, and Alfie had that with knobs on, but me, love? I much prefer a man with a present!'

'I thought Herb was your brother?'

'Not blood, but he might as well have bin. In fact, it was Herb who suggested I change my stage name when we moved to the Smoke. I put in to be a Gaiety Girl, see, but when Mr.

Edwardes, that's the owner of the Gaiety Theatre, didn't give me a spot, Herb said if I called myself Gigi — Gaiety Girl, GG, get it? — other theatre owners would blithely assume I'd danced in his chorus. Got in to all manner of musical comedies after that.'

'Do you still dance?'

'Lord, no. Gave up the leaps and high kicks a while back.' Dora patted her pearls. 'Came into some money and decided that were enough flashing me thighs to dirty old men. Not that I don't miss it.' She tipped her head on one side and laughed. 'Till you've run round a stage in your skimpies, titillating the audience and shocking 'em in equal measures, you haven't lived. Wild times, love, I tell you. Wild times.' She leaned forward. 'Could've had me pick of any number of swells. You see 'em at all the best restaurants, these Gaiety Girls. You see 'em at Ascot and Henley, and it would knock your eyes out how many end up marrying into money and titles, but me. I was married already, and that, as they say, was that.'

'Sounds exciting. I can see why you miss it — ah! Sergeant!'

*Not before bloody time.* Julia's stock of small talk was running perilously low. 'Mrs. Pike here —'

'Dora, love.'

'Dora has also identified your first robbery victim. Herbert Pike, her husband's cousin.'

'Blimey.' Kincaid looked like he'd been poleaxed for a second time, only this time without his trusty bowler hat to protect him. 'My condolences, Mrs. Pike, and as much as I hate to trouble you, this must be a terrible shock I do realise, but in light of that revelation, I'm afraid I'll need to take another statement.' He followed Julia back into the mortuary. 'Sorry I wasted your time here, but might I have word after I've finished with Mrs. Pike?'

'I'll be in the dispensary.'

The dispensary was an equally depressing sector, but at least the inmates would be breathing, because whichever way Julia turned in this hideous dungeon, the Grim Reaper's breath was cold on her neck, and the bastard seemed to be revelling in it. Passing the nurses' sitting room and a chamber where at least a dozen doctors and nurses clustered round a patient to administer a blood transfusion, Julia thought of the effect of steam on the hospital since four silver coins were solemnly placed beneath its first foundation stone, and the bells of St. Oswald's rang for three hours to mark the occasion. There were no factories back then. No mills. No refineries. No railways. Not even this arm of the Grand Union Canal. That didn't come until twenty years later. The hospital was a simple two-storey building, where cattle grazed the surrounding fields, there were gardens on the south side, and the staff consisted of an apothecary, his assistant, a matron, a porter, a cook, three nurses, a secretary and housemaid, with the senior staff receiving bonus payments for sugar and tea. There were just forty-four iron beds.

One the pace of industrialisation picked up, though, everything changed. Fields vanished beneath belching chimneys and densely packed tenements. Typhoid, smallpox, tuberculosis and cholera spread like wildfire, resulting in the construction of the Fever House, with two wards for patients suffering from venereal disease, where the doors were kept permanently locked. As the factories multiplied, so did industrial accidents. Nearly a thousand last year alone. Another storey was promptly added, along with two additional wings, and while vaccination contained certain diseases, notably scarlet fever, such was the massive increase in population that today the hospital boasted four wings off the main building and well over two hundred beds. Needless to say the gardens were long gone.

'Sorry to keep you hanging around, only I wanted to talk to Mrs. Pike first. Double bereavement, and all that. Shall we sit?'

'Do you think we'll find room, Sergeant?'

Like the morgue, the dispensary was another vaulted dungeon approached by steps leading down. Thanks to row upon row of wooden benches seating twenty lined up like pews and an open gallery with wrought iron railings, it looked like a church and felt like a prison. During the week, this place would be busier than Victoria train station but today, being Sunday, the dispensary was closed, meaning they were the only two in this cavernous hall.

Still they spoke in hushed tones.

'Thing is, Miss, I have a favour to ask.'

*Anything,* Julia thought. *Just make it quick.*

The only natural light came from a semi-circular window at the "altar" end of the hall, casting the galleries into twilight where amputees on crutches groaned with the pain, babies cried, cripples hopped, nurses clopped, every sound echoing round the empty hall and mingling with its counterpart like hungry ghosts.

'Saturday night's always a busy time for Boot Street. Robberies, brawls, violations against women, I'm sure you don't need me to draw pictures, and last night was no exception. With that lot to contend with, on top of these two latest murders, our resources are stretched to breaking point.'

'Especially with your Chief Inspector — indisposed.'

'You know about that?' Kincaid pulled out his pipe, thought of lighting it, then tucked it back in his pocket. 'Then I'd be obliged if you'd keep it information to yourself, but what I'm saying is, what with everything coming at once, we've had no chance to follow up on your Rowena. Rather, Mary Mason, to give her her proper name now.'

'Where exactly do I fit in?'

'Ah. Well. Since her lodgings are for women only, I was wondering if you'd mind going along instead of us doing it, Miss? Girl-to-girl, it'll be easier to elicit information, anyway.'

Julia took the key found in Mary Mason's reticule, along with a piece of paper on which Kincaid had scribbled her address. 'Is this my punishment for taking you back to square one with the motive for her murder?'

'Y'know, I really thought I'd cracked it with that one, then along comes Mrs. Female Perspective, saying a bully needs to dominate his victim to the end and blows my theory out the water.' He laughed. 'So yeah. Bloody right this is payback.' He lit his pipe as he stood up. 'I'm still grateful.'

Female perspective her arse. This was all down to experience, because abuse makes you watchful, even as a small child. You soon learn how to read situations, then how to read people, searching for the smallest changes in their movements or facial expressions to signal what's coming next. Every night Julia went to sleep, hoping her stepfather would change, willing him to change, praying for him to change. People like him never do, though, that's the thing. The wickedness only continues to grow. As does hate.

The irony was, all through her childhood, she'd been terrified her stepfather would kill either her mother, her brother or herself — and what happens? Julia ends up the killer in the family. She becomes the evil one, not him. Charles Darwin shocked the world thirty-six years ago, propounding his theory of evolution and survival of the fittest. Charles Darwin was wrong.

It was survival of the smartest.

Aaron studied his reflection. A few lines — quite a few lines — in his face since he first went on the run, and he was so skinny, his mother would cry.

He'd prayed for them last night. Poppa. His mother. All the people he'd loved and let down. He'd prayed and he'd cried, begging for forgiveness that could never be given, but the past was the past was the past.

Taking a deep breath, Aaron picked up his hat.

Time to pay his respects on the widow.

# Chapter 24

Walking down the broad, tree-lined avenue that would take her to Mary Mason's lodging house, her skirts swishing through the first falling leaves, Julia pictured her new life, with a new identity. Oh, the freedom, the relief, not having to constantly look over her shoulder. Not having to pretend her employer was making a home visit. Not having to flog china dogs to keep the business afloat. It would be different, certainly, not having roots, but exciting. Travelling the Silk Road. Taking ships round both Horns. Photographing mountains that made Ben Nevis look like a pimple, and rivers that made the Thames seem a trickle.

Gradually, streets lined with stucco houses with Italianate features and garden squares gave way to more modest terraced accommodation, but none of it compared to the other side of the canal, where overcrowding, poverty, violence and disease prospered. Washing hung across the street from every upstairs window, even though it was the Lord's day. Quarrels raged over nothing, dogs barked, babies bawled, beggars whined, and there'd be no swishing leaves as she walked. Luckily, Julia didn't need to lift her hem to navigate the alleys. Mary Mason's lodging house sat firmly on this side of the bridge, a four-storey red brick building with tall Queen Anne windows and a potted gold dust plant by the door. Its neatness and respectability brought a sudden lump to Julia's throat, as she saw again the neat darns in the camisole ... the carefully pressed, if faded, drawers...

'Sorry to trouble you,' she told the landlady, 'on a Sunday,' she added, noting the prominent gold cross at her neck, 'but I was wondering if you'd rented Mary Mason's accommodation yet.' Julia phrased it carefully. *Was it Miss Mason, was Mrs? One room? Two?* 'The thing is, I'm looking to rent myself, and Mary speaks very highly of you. Unfortunately, with her off to New York on Tuesday and so much to sort out, our paths didn't cross at the right time for her to show me round herself.' *Smile, smile, show lots of teeth.* 'Instead, she gave me her key and suggested I took a look on my own. Is that all right? I mean, obviously you can accompany me. Make sure I don't steal anything.'

She needn't have bothered with the charade. The landlady didn't care she might be a thief in silk clothing (perhaps there was nothing worth pinching), or that she may or may not be a friend, and she wasn't won over by good manners or flattery either. Julia had her at the word "rent".

'Yours from the end of the week, if you want it. Second floor, top of the stairs on the left.'

None of this was what Julia had been expecting. The room was tiny but it had cheerful chintz curtains, a deep piled rug, a pink quilted eiderdown and feather pillows. The dresser was narrow from necessity, but it still boasted three deep drawers and two small ones, side by side, plus a table with pretty Delft jug and bowl. All the way over, Julia had ghastly visions of a hovel so dark that Mary would have had to grope her way up the stairs, guiding her way with her hands on the wall. That Mary, poor and destitute since she was unable to afford new underclothes, had fallen into prostitution (or whatever it was that lured her to the back of the Apollo) as a last resort. Of course, that might still be the case, and Mary had rated her digs above dignity.

Sadly, dignity no longer had a part in this play.

'Sorry, Mary.' Julia hefted the heavy leather suitcase onto the bed. 'I know it must feel like I'm prying, but I do need to go through your things.'

God willing, this was the last humiliation Mary would suffer. A stranger rummaging through treasured possessions in the form of a hand mirror and hairbrush with pretty embroidery on the back under glass, a perfume bottle, empty, but clearly loved or it wouldn't be on its way to New York, a batch of curled, faded photographs. Julia turned them over. Most of them read things like *Grandad's Garden* or *Auntie Bertha* on the back. One, though, said *Mum, Dad, me & Sid, Margate, '65*. In it, little Mary looked about six years old, which would make her thirty-five, thirty-six when she died. Hopefully that should narrow things down for the police, but there was nothing to trace the victim back to her family. Not so much as a bundle of letters.

*Mary, Mary, what's going on here? Did you lose track of your family through accident? Through design?*

Had she thrown the letters away? Or not received any because she had no one to write to? The only papers were passport, handwritten details of the timings of her passage, an address in New York, either a contact, friend or lodgings, together with a receipt from the travel agency on Cadogan Street who'd booked her the one-way ticket.

A lump formed in Julia's throat. Was that the sum total of Mary Mason's life? Was she, God forbid, another Julia McAllister? Always looking over her shoulder? Always on the run? Until the past finally catches up at the back of a derelict theatre…?

'Thank goodness, love! I worried you'd left without saying goodbye — ooh sorry, I thought it was Mary.' The face that bobbed round the door was young, freckled and framed by a

Salvation Army bonnet tied in a big bow at the side of her neck. 'Amazing, really. We only live across the hall from one another, but talk about ships that pass in the night. If we missed each other once, we must've missed each other half a dozen times this week, but I'd hate to let her go without saying cheerio and wishing her luck. Break a leg, isn't that what you lot say?'

'Us ... lot?'

'You're not from the theatricals, then? Only with them lovely clothes and you packing up her stuff, well, I assumed her all friends was actors. I'm glad, by the way.'

'That she's leaving, or that all her friends are actors?'

'No. Glad. Short for Gladys.'

'Julia.' They shook hands. 'To be honest I've never met Mary.' If she told Gladys her neighbour was dead, she'd flip into prayer and salvation mode, and Julia would learn nothing. 'I'm just friend of a friend helping out.' She dangled the key. 'Seeing how the steamer leaves the day after tomorrow and there's so much to do.'

Glad's freckles puckered in disappointment. 'Spose this means I won't see her again?'

'I think that's a safe bet.'

'Pity, 'cause although our paths didn't cross often — me working in the fabric shop and spending all my spare time on relief work for the poor, her employed in the tea rooms down by the Arcade and taking any acting she could get — she was a scream, that girl. She has everyone in this boarding house in stitches. I know you've never met her, but if you get the chance, love, grab it. 'Cause I tell you, she only has to look at you once, and you could walk down them stairs and before you got to the bottom step, she'll have you off pat. Walk, mannerisms, voice, the whole bleedin' works.' She lowered her voice to a whisper. 'I know us Salvationists aren't supposed to say it, acting being ... you know...'

'Sinful?'

'The lifestyle anyway, but Mary? She's so talented, Broadway will love her, and I tell you, this house will be a duller place without her, that's for sure.'

'Is the whole production moving to New York?'

'Oh, no, nothing like that, and that's the trouble. No parts in the theatre for women on the wrong side of thirty. That's why she's so excited. The Americans aren't half as snobby. They look for talent, and our Mary has that in spades. If you get to meet her, ask about the tea shop. Honestly! The way she takes off management and customers will make your sides ache, and the other thing, if you do happen to see her, tell her Glad really hopes she gets the big break she deserves. Ooh, crikey. Look at the time. Must dash or I'll be late for the Meeting! Bye!'

It was all Julia could do not to punch the air and waltz as she retraced her steps down the tree-lined avenues back to the studio. This visit might not have solved Mary's murder, but it was enough to put the police on the right track. Forget obsessive boyfriends and controlling bullies. This bore every hallmark of professional jealousy, and the fact that she was killed at the Apollo wasn't coincidence.

Julia could take that train, happy in the knowledge that she'd been instrumental in giving an anonymous victim her name back, and that, all things being equal, this was no longer one of those murders where the odds of being solved were hundreds to one. And with no greater spotlight for an actor than a trial at the Old Bailey, it might even be said that confession is good for the role.

# Chapter 25

'John?'

Collingwood unravelled himself from Julia's blue velvet sofa, tossing the Sunday *Chronicle* to one side. 'I'm sorry if you think I regard your place as my personal retreat, but —'

He had nowhere else to go. She understood. 'The Double Act wouldn't take "no" for an answer?'

'Your little grey lodgers are very persuasive. I only wish the villains who pass through my interrogation room talked as much as those two.'

'For all their chatter, they say nothing, so the end result is the same.'

'They say a lot of nice things about you.'

'Who doesn't.'

Collingwood's haggard features almost made the journey to a smile. 'For instance, they can't speak highly enough about the way you bumped into the insurance man. As a consequence, I gather he wrote them a juicy, fat cheque for structural renovations.'

'So?'

'Then there's the furniture you've earmarked for them. The sofa I've just been sitting on, for example. The sideboard, the dresser —'

'They exaggerate.'

'The crockery. The cutlery. The linens.'

'They drink.'

'Anyone would think you were leaving for good.'

How could Julia have been so stupid as to leave her passport and papers lying around? Had he seen her satchel? The blue and gold carpet bag? It came naturally to policemen to poke inside things. Julia squared her shoulders. She had two choices. Meet the challenge in Collingwood's grey wolf eyes. Or —

'I confess, Inspector. You've got me bang to rights. I drink, as well. Had I been sober, I wouldn't have drawn up that list.'

'Had I been sober, I wouldn't have proposed to my wife.'

Collingwood was trying to make light of it, but he didn't fool Julia. So far, she'd made a bloody good fist of covering up her involvement in the dirty picture trade. Every search he'd made of her studio had come up empty, making her, in theory, the model of propriety. Providing the old rented rooms remained a secret, there was no imminent threat, and in any case, it wasn't a criminal offence to take pornographic photographs, only in the possession and distribution of same, and she'd burned every trace. But one carelessly dropped word, and Julia's world would tumble like a house of cards.

Thanks to him, she'd missed the afternoon train, but come hell or high water, she'd be heading to London first thing in the morning.

'Harrington telephoned.' Collingwood paced the parlour like a caged tiger. 'Sunday or not, he's rushing this through. Tomorrow morning, Emily will be escorted to Broadmoor, at which point it becomes incumbent upon me to ensure she spends the rest of her life there.'

Julia shivered. *Straightjackets. Bromide. Cold baths. Electroconvulsive therapy. Lobotomies.* She'd hang before spending the rest of her life in an asylum.

'What happened is not your fault, John, but the good thing is that she's their responsibility now, and not yours.'

'The hell it is.' Collingwood looked at her as though she was a child. 'Every doctor wants to cure their patient, Julia, and psychiatrists are no exception.'

'Don't you want her cured?'

'If I thought it was possible, then yes. Absolutely.' He cradled the coffee cup. 'Otherwise, I'd spend my whole life doing what I'm doing now. Wondering if Alice would have turned out the same way as her mother. Chip off the old block, and all that.'

'There are two blocks, don't forget that.'

His tortured eyes smiled his thanks. 'Asylum doctors believe moral treatment combined with discipline and a strong father figure is the cure for what they term lunacy. This means Emily could be discharged at any time into the care of a relative or a friend, if such an application is made and I need to make sure that doesn't happen. No one knows her like I do, and now that I know what she's capable of, I also know the signs to watch out for.'

'Southolt's only six miles away. Surely their beds aren't full?'

'Oh, there's room. Plenty of room. Just not on a policeman's wages. Even if I sell the house, there's too great a shortfall, and on my pay, the bank won't lend me the money I'd need. Anyway!' He rubbed both hands briskly together. 'Enough of my problems. How did you get on at Mary Mason's?'

Julia couldn't keep the elation out of her voice as she relayed her conversation with the freckled Salvationist and outlined her theory about Mary's attacker.

'You think it's a woman?'

'I do.' It explained why Mary was hit from behind. Most women aren't violent by nature, and even those who are tend to be squeamish when it comes to blood, brains and bone. 'Professional jealousy, I'd bet my best hat on it. That's why she buried her lovely silk clothes. No doubt Mary bought them to impress New York theatre owners, only in the killer's eyes, they represented the ultimate symbol of her rival's success.

You'll find her easily enough. She's the one who will be boasting how she's the better actress.'

They were looking for someone who bitterly resented her rival's determination to never give up, and hated that she had the guts to start a new life on the other side of the Atlantic and would probably break through. Someone who wanted to bring her down a peg and rub her nose in it. That very arrogance will give the murderer away, and unless they were habitual criminals, women were pretty quick to crack. By the time Julia was in Paris, Mary Mason's killer would be waiting to stand trial, and relishing every second of the limelight. A star at last!

'Female perspective. Can't beat it.' Collingwood reached for his hat. 'Now, as much as I prize this delightful refuge from criminals who spend so much time questioning my parentage and throwing up in the cells, Boot Street calls. First thing in the morning, I'll set Charlie off to *cherchez la femme*, but right now, Dora Pike is top priority.'

'Good God, don't tell me she's been attacked —'

'No. It's just that we're pretty sure she orchestrated the hits on the Pike boys. We just need to prove it.'

'What makes you think that?'

'Call it instinct, call it a hunch, but something's not right. Alf was a pickpocket and a thief in his younger days, served time in Strangeways and Pentonville, to name but two, and never had a job that we know of. As for Herb, the only thing we're sure of here is that he was a gambler, and I've never known gamblers have two pennies to rub together without betting both of them on cards or a horse. The Pikes, all three from — let's say humble backgrounds — have been living high on the hog, staying in top notch hotels like the Grand and, you saw yourself, those clothes didn't come cheap. So yes. I'd very

203

much like to ask the lovely Dora where the funding comes from.'

'She told me she came into some money.'

'She told Charlie the same thing, but there's no record of an inheritance to back up her story. What really set off warning bells,' he added, 'was how Dora was shocked, but not distraught. Saddened, but not surprised and, to put it bluntly, not desperately put out.'

Funnily enough, now he mentioned it, Julia was inclined to agree. Dora had literally only just identified her husband's body, before discovering her husband's cousin had also been beaten to death — yet she had wits enough about her to take in Julia's profession and consider her "one of the sisterhood". Everyone grieves in different ways, of course, and maybe the double tragedy hadn't yet sunk in. But while Alfie and Herb cropped up in conversation, Dora's prime interest was very much Dora.

'I might be able to help with that, Detective Inspector.'

'And how might that be, Mrs. McAllister?'

'She obviously felt comfortable with me, and because she's probably starved of female company since giving up the stage, I suspect that's the reason she opened up. Now if that's in the mortuary immediately after identifying her loved ones, imagine what she'd let slip, if I were to call round and, say, check that she's all right...'

Collingwood stopped pacing. 'You have another theory, don't you?'

'More passing thought than theory, but — well. What if the two men in the morgue aren't Alf and Herb, but two lookalikes? Why else would their features need to be obliterated? It also explains why Dora wasn't brought to her knees.'

For the first time in a long time, Collingwood laughed. 'Told you you'd missed your vocation.'

'I thought that was photography, not detective work?'

'When you first showed me your dark room and I said "so that's where the magic is made", you were quick to gun me down. You pointed to your heart and told me that was where the magic was made. Later, you talked about wanting to capture wild places and wild weather, then use the latest photographic techniques to superimpose exotic creatures on these scenes, so that people who don't have access to the Natural History Museum can see them in their natural habitat.'

'That flame still burns.' *Indeed, it would get its chance to shine very, very soon.*

'And these photographs on your walls.' He tapped a seemingly peaceful agricultural scene of workers enjoying a picnic in the shade of a haystack. 'Am I right in thinking this was an amalgam of four different images, overlaid one on the other, to create the right picture?'

'Five images, and no. The aim is to recreate, not invent. In this case, the light wasn't right, they didn't stay still long enough, and moving composition isn't like a portrait in the studio.'

'Exactly. You have a subject, you become involved in the picture.'

'Professional pride, John. We all have it.'

'The same professional pride that made you name a corpse Rowena to render her human again?'

'I felt sorry for her then, and I still do.'

'You were drawn to the victim, you wanted justice for her and, like those men in the field, except on a much larger scale, you wanted her story to be told.'

'Is that so wrong?'

'On the contrary, except now you're drawn to the Pike boys, and why? Because you've seen them — met them, if you like — and good men or bad, you care about them.'

'What's your point?'

'That you've finally understood what I've known all along. Every victim matters.'

The Grand Hotel was aptly named. If four opulent storeys topped by a domed tower, like a miniature St. Paul's, wasn't enough to cow the public, the silence inside was. From the second the liveried doorman swept off his top hat in a generous bow, every crack of the cab driver's whip and every creak of the delivery boy's barrow, every shout, whinny, winch and whistle became lost to carpets so thick that ankles disappeared, below panelled ceilings so high that mountain goats would turn dizzy.

Julia navigated her way to the lift past buttoned sofas and padded easy chairs, mahogany desks and inlaid writing tables, each so far from its neighbour you'd need a telescope to see them. Staff in maroon and gold glided like ghosts, delivering drinks, calling cards, messages and letters on gleaming silver trays.

The lift wasn't for the drunk and disorderly, being one of the open-box, constantly moving affairs known as paternosters. Then again, the Grand's clientele weren't exactly the drunk and disorderly kind, and in any case, the hotel probably employed flunkies whose sole role was to scoop them up with calm and discretion.

Upstairs was equally sumptuous. As legions of chambermaids scurried and cleaned, it gave Julia the chance to peep into the bedrooms where the shine on the brass bedsteads was enough to make a dray horse bolt, and the gold on the friezes put Egyptian mummies to shame.

Room sixty-two, Collingwood had said.

Julia was about to knock, when she noticed the door was ajar, as though pushed closed, just not hard enough for it to click shut by itself. Putting her ear to the crack, she heard voices. A man and a woman's. The voices were low, the woman's especially — muffled, as though she was contradicting her companion through a mouth full of toast.

Something kicked in Julia's chest. She tried not to consider that it might be a kick of excitement. 'Got you,' she said, breezing into the room.

Except she hadn't.

In a hard-backed chair by the bed, Dora Pike sat bloodied, bound and gagged. Behind her, a skinny individual, with a mass of thick curly hair and a broken spectacle lens, had his tie wrapped round her throat and was pulling hard with both hands.

# Chapter 26

'Look, it-it-it's not what you think.'

'What I think is that you barged your way in when Mrs. Pike opened the door,' Julia told the man. 'I think she tried to fight you off, but you're strong and wiry, you overpowered her, tied her up and, unless my eyes deceive me, I think you're intent on strangling her.'

'I wanted her to tell me she's sorry.'

'She'd be in a better position to say it without a silk stocking in her mouth, so if you don't mind, you stand perfectly still, please, while I call the police. If you move, I will shoot you.'

Julia's voice was as steady as the British Bull Dog revolver in her hand.

'Please. Hear me out first.' He nodded towards the bottle of pills he'd placed on the dresser. 'I'm going to kill myself anyway. I need to tell someone. Someone needs to hear my story. Then you can shoot me.'

*There's a woman. She's a dancer. The chorus line is the perfect showcase for a beautiful girl with tight blonde curls, curvaceous thighs and a bubbly personality. She loves to dance, she loves the music, she loves the limelight, too.*

*She spots a man in the audience, same seat every night, right at the front. She smiles at the man in the same seat every night, right at the front. From then on, he has eyes for no other girl on the stage.*

*He learns her name. Gigi. He sends her notes. He sends her flowers. He sends her a beautiful dragonfly brooch set with rubies, diamonds and sapphires. He waits at the stage door. Steps forward nervously.*

*'Can I buy you dinner?'*

*The dancer nods. She links her arm with his, and from then on, life is good. They dine, they dance, they do this for three nights, then they fall into bed, and then they fall in love. He is a jeweller, on the road to secure commissions. She is married, but she daren't tell him this. She merely hints at the drunk who knocked seven bells out of her so often and so badly that she had to leave Manchester and is too terrified to return.*

*One night, in her hotel room, they are kissing when there's a loud banging on her door. It's the man she ran away from, and he is steaming drunk and furious. He barges in. Grabs Gigi's hair. The jeweller doesn't hesitate. He picks up a chair and swings it, knocks the boyfriend to the floor. Sobbing, Gigi tells the man to go. Go, and never come back, there's no point. She is marrying the love of her life. Growling threats, the man staggers out. Neither of them pay him the slightest attention.*

*'Did you mean it?' Aaron asks breathlessly. 'You want to marry me?'*

*'You know I do,' she says, hugging him. 'In fact, let's do it right now, right this minute! Take the train to Gretna Green and get a licence first thing in the morning.'*

*Again, she doesn't mention the licence that binds her to Alfred Pike. Does it matter? They're in love. Whatever problems lay ahead, they will face them together.*

*'I love you so much, Aaron. I really do.'*

*The jeweller races to his own room. Starts throwing clothes in the suitcase. He hears a shot —*

*Running back, Gigi is slumped on the floor, covered with blood and the boyfriend is standing over her with a gun. Realising there's no escape through the door, he throws down the weapon and runs to the window.*

*'Gigi, no!' Aaron rushes forward. Cradles her in his arms. She is fighting for breath. So is he. 'No, Gigi, no!'*

*'Kill him, Aaron.' Through the death rattle, she finds the strength to press the revolver into his hand. 'Don't ... let me ... die ... unavenged.'*

*With her last breath, tells him she loves him.*

*The jeweller is distraught. It is a moment before he realises there's a man in the corridor, a guest, with key poised, about to enter the room opposite, whose mouth is open in horror.*

*'Murder!' he croaks.*

*He is too shocked to shout. The sound won't come out.*

*'Murder!'*

*'No, no, it wasn't me!' The bereaved lover drops the gun and points to the window. 'The killer escaped through the window. Look, if you don't believe me!'*

*The guest peers down the empty street. Looks at the bloodstained jeweller. Puts his head out the window and yells. 'MURDER!"*

*Instantly, a police whistle sounds.*

*'Gotcha!' The guest makes a grab for his collar. 'Red handed, you bastard.'*

*'Y-y-you don't understand —'*

*'I'll see you hanged for this, you scoundrel.'*

*The whistle is close. Aaron panics. Diving through the window, he follows Gigi's killer down the fire escape and into the night.*

In this grand room in the Grand Hotel, there was silence. Nothing but the sound of the clock on the dresser, ticking away the final dregs of Aaron's life. The final dregs of his hope.

'You have to believe me,' he said. 'I thought she was dead. I heard the last breath leave her body. I'd left my wallet and the sample case containing my precious stones in the hotel room. I couldn't go back, the police would be waiting, and I couldn't go home. I went from being happy, wealthy and in love, to having no money, no career, no prospects. Nothing. You don't know what it's like. The loneliness. The emptiness. Five years trapped in a rat-infested, puke-ridden hell, my family in agony, believing their son was a killer, me believing my true love was dead and the police were hunting me.

'But then, on Wednesday, I spotted Gigi in the Arcade. There was no mistaking that swing of the hips. The way my darling girl tips her head on one side. For two days, I couldn't think of anything else. I lost my job on account of it, but all I could think of was how I'd abandoned her when she needed me most. What kind of bastard does that? But, if I spruced myself up, and threw myself on her mercy, Gigi would understand. She'd loved me. With all her heart, with all her soul, she'd said. She would forgive me, and God willing, we might start again. Then I saw her. Outside the restaurant.' It took a few gulping breaths for Aaron to pull himself together enough to continue. 'Laughing with two men I would know anywhere.'

*Of course. The "drunken bully of a boyfriend", and the "witness" in the hall.*

Keeping the revolver levelled at the man gripping the tie round Dora's neck, Julia removed the gag.

She knew what it was like. The loneliness. The emptiness. Never letting anyone close. Not because you might inadvertently let something slip. That's too ingrained. You don't build friendships or let people into your heart, because you know you will have to move on and leave them. There are only so many times you can be hurt.

'Is that where the money came from?' she asked.

Dora's eyes bulged, but not from the ligature. It was disbelief. 'Don't tell me you swallowed this lunatic's lies?'

'Just answer the question. Was it the sale of Aaron's diamonds that allowed you to quit the chorus line?'

'I got too old, love. You know a girl can't dance past twenty-five, never mind thirty.'

'What about the string of luxury hotels? The latest fashions? The most expensive fabrics money can buy?'

Julia doubted Aaron was the first mark, but she'd bet he was the last, and the game would have been the same every time. The perfect three-person con trick.

Number One targets a man in the audience, starting with the ones who take the same seat every night, then she smiles at him in such a way that he has eyes for no one else. She makes sure he learns her name. That she's not averse to receiving flowers, notes and gifts. In no time, he joins the line of stage door johnnies. They dine, they dance, they fall in bed, they fall in love. Or at least one of them does.

Shortly into the relationship, while still heady from infatuation, Number Two "the drunk who knocked seven bells out of her" turns up out of the blue. Our hero has been well primed to step in and save the day, prompting the old let's-elope line. He rushes off to pack, setting the stage for the final act, in which a gun goes off and Gigi plays the dying swan.

Cue an innocent stranger, Number Three, to pass the open doorway, catching her killer covered in pig's blood, gun in his hand, kneeling over the body.

'I'm guessing one of two scenarios play out here, Dora. Either the witness shakes down your lover for money or he'll call the police. At which point, once your lover has coughed up, it's you who skedaddles out the window. Or, like Aaron's case, the drunken bully — I'm thinking Alfie — runs up the fire escape, not down, which is how the street is empty. And it's Alf who blows the whistle, making it appear the police are almost on the scene. After which, it's a simple case of robbing his hotel room.'

'This is nonsense, love,' Dora told Julia. 'He's making it up. I told you, I came into some money. I've never seen this man in my life —'

'She's lying,' Aaron interrupted.

'I agree,' Julia replied, 'but you killing her then killing yourself was never the right way to end it, Aaron.'

'Ira. I'm Ira now. Ira Miller.' Tears streamed down his face. 'She killed Aaron when she ripped his heart out.'

'You're the killer!' Dora was adamant. 'You killed my husband and my brother —'

'I gave them a chance. Both of them.' Aaron was talking to Julia, not Dora. 'But the first one, he looked me up and down and he sneered. Actually curled his lip. So what? he said, when I confronted him under the bridge. You're a dosser, a loser, you stink like a sewer and look like a turd. No one's interested in your sob story, pal. No one'll believe you, because the three of us will swear different. He said if I went back to the hotel I would find there was never any record of a murder. Not even of shots fired. He had the gall to boast about it. How the lady slipped the night clerk a few bob, saying she wanted to play a practical joke on a friend, keep it to himself and she'd see him right.

'The hotel register showed that I left early to catch the milk train. The desk clerk wasn't on shift when I checked in, so he saw no reason to doubt the man who was checking out, and that's when I snapped,' Aaron said. 'I'd been picked out purely for being gentle and mild. Those three planned the scam like a military campaign. They left me to rot without a shred of remorse, and then mocked me for it.

'The second one, I gave him every chance, too. I said we could still go to the police, come clean, take our chances, and you know what he said? He said, "My cousin spins the roulette wheel twelve times a night, old son. He'd be the first to say them's not good odds." That's when I beat the grin off his face. So, do it. Pull the trigger,' Aaron begged Julia. 'Sleeping pills might only make me ill, but a bullet's final. Do it, or I swear I'll kill her.'

'You're not a killer.' Julia's gaze didn't waver from the tortured eyes of the jeweller as she lowered the gun and tucked it back inside her reticule. Damn thing wasn't loaded, anyway. 'If you'd wanted to kill Dora, you'd have done it long before I came on the scene.'

'I told you. I wanted to hear her say she was sorry.'

'Ah, well, that's the thing, she won't. None of them would, they don't understand the meaning of compassion, it isn't in them.' That's why Dora was cold calm in the morgue, Julia thought. She had been shocked, but not distraught. Many times she'd have mooted the possibility that one day things could go wrong, but unlike Aaron, she lacked the ability to love. Her sole core value was self-preservation.

Aaron's shoulders heaved as he dropped the tie on the floor. Julia whisked the bottle of pills from his hand and dropped them in her reticule, alongside the revolver.

'If you'd killed yourself, you'd have died the man these people made you. If I was in your shoes I'd prefer to be the man I was before they ruined my life.'

'You think the executioner cares what kind of killer he hangs?' Aaron asked.

Julia opened the writing desk, every bit as grand as the rest of the hotel. Inside, as she'd expected, was a ledger, because she'd bet this happy trio took great pleasure in crowing over the power they held. There was a perfect set of books that that listed nineteen names, including Aaron Adelman, against which was the amount they'd fleeced each of their marks for.

'We all have to die some time, Aaron. I just don't see any reason why you shouldn't stretch your span for another thirty years.'

'I can't face a cell.'

'Who's asking you to?'

'What?' Dora squirmed inside the rope he'd brought along to bind her. 'You're not letting him go! You ... you ... you can't do this! This little bastard killed my brother and my husband! You can't let him walk off scot free!'

'You can't go home,' Julia said levelly, ignoring Dora. 'Not now, not ever. Funds or no funds in your safety deposit box, there's no way back for Aaron Adelman.' She paused. 'There is a way forward Ira Miller, though.'

'Are you mad?' Dora shouted. 'He butchered two men, then came to kill me!'

'Is this some kind of trap? Are you one them?' Aaron didn't understand. 'Who are you, anyway?'

'Who I am doesn't matter. What does, is that I'm giving you a chance to start over.'

'This isn't right,' Dora wailed.

'Probably not, but neither's what you three drove him to,' Julia snapped, 'and while I don't condone what he did, I understand why he was driven to do it. The way I see it, Dora, there's as much blood on your hands as there is on Aaron's, so here's the choice — we either take this to the police, and while I'm not sure how much satisfaction watching Aaron hanged will give you, you'll have fifteen years of hard labour to mull it over —'

'Oh, no, no, I can't,' Dora gasped. 'I can't go to prison. Aaron, darling, please. I'm sorry for what I put you through, and I'm sorry I lied to you, but it was Alf. He made me do it. You saw him, that night he attacked me in the room — I love you, Aaron. I always have. I'm sorry I said those things just now, I was scared, but he can start again, just like we said we would. I'm a widow. We can get married legally —'

'Aaron Adelman might have fallen for that line, Gigi. But not me. Not Ira Miller.'

'Sweetheart. Please.' Dora wasn't giving up. 'You know I'm too delicate for prison.'

'But not,' Julia said, 'too delicate to sign a confession in exchange for your own freedom.'

Julia typed it up. Dora signed. Aaron compared it to other signatures in the desk to be sure.

'I'll be lodging this with my solicitor,' Julia lied — tomorrow she would be on the train heading for London, then Paris, then who knows where next. It didn't stop her adding that if Dora tried anything like this again, conning people out of what was rightfully theirs, this confession would go straight to the police and Julia would personally see she rotted in jail. She'd turned to Aaron. 'You still have your talent?'

'I do.'

'Then put it to use,' Julia said, handing him Dora's jewellery box.

# Chapter 27

'Tickets, please!' The inspector studied Julia's ticket, clipped it, then returned it with a smile. 'Thank you, Miss. Have a good journey.'

Glancing at her cases squashed into the overhead luggage rack, Julia knew she would.

Rocked by the rhythmic rattle of the rails, she settled back into her window seat. It was not quite up to Queen Victoria's standards, where the carriage walls were padded with silk, but comfortable enough, although her departure wasn't either as smooth or early as she'd hoped. It was annoying just how much there was to sort out in the end, especially after her unscheduled visits to Mary Mason's lodgings and then Dora.

'You're sure Dora didn't orchestrate the hits on the Pike boys?' Kincaid asked in the first of the seemingly hundreds of telephone calls she'd had to make.

'Absolutely positive, Sergeant. She is genuinely distraught.' Not necessarily in the way he might think, but she'd lost everything but her freedom, and that hung only by a thread. 'Transpires her husband and his cousin were a pair of con artists, whose past finally caught up with them. That's where the money was coming from. Dora admitted she knew what they were up to, but it seems her husband was a drunk and a bully, who knocked seven bells out of her. She was too terrified to leave him or go to the police.' With the ledger and confession tucked away in Julia's case, Dora would be sticking to the script like a bloody limpet. 'Their killers are probably on their way back to Manchester as we speak.'

Before Kincaid's gravelly thanks had stopped ringing in her ears, Julia had turned to the next item on her checklist, until finally it was a hansom to the station, and this time there was no Irish tornado around to make her miss the train.

*Yer'll not catching me being tied to one place. Roving reporter, that's Orla Keane, because interesting stories cover any manner of distance, and crime don't have a conscience about straying past police boundaries, that it does not.*

Only a blind man could live in Oakbourne without reading about killings, beatings and robberies in the papers. The combination of canals, industrialisation and gentrified living was a combustible one and it was only a few short weeks ago that murder and betrayal had knocked on Julia's own door, ripping her life and her heart into shreds. But how often had she stopped to think what might be happening beyond these boundaries?

As a photographer, taking portraits and selling china dogs to make ends meet, fighting to retain her independence through the dirty picture trade, her life was full, yet, as she'd discovered yesterday, surprisingly narrow. And while she was keenly aware of "random acts of violence" and even with the tragic circumstances of Collingwood's daughter and the death of Mary, Julia had been so focussed on finding justice for the victim that she'd overlooked the fact that hundreds of other lives up and down the country were equally shattered, often beyond mending.

*You can't change the past, but you can influence the future, JJ.*

Wise words from a wise man. Time to look to the future, not to the past. Time, at last, to start a new life.

Within no time, sooty streets heaving with rat catchers, costermongers, chimney sweeps and crawlers gave way to farmlands, orchards and fields. Oakbourne might be within spitting distance of its neighbours and London, and the gaps between might be closing, but there were no beggars maimed from faulty machinery here. No children twisted from malnutrition. Whose spirits wouldn't be lifted by these vast green open spaces, where smoke wasn't belching out from chimneys to darken the sky, but where fields and trees stretched to infinity, rabbits hopped by the hedgerows and the only thing that clattered were magpies?

Thanks to the railways cutting both time and costs, factories paid considerably more than farm work, to the point where there was not enough labour to adequately manage the land, and the balance grew worse every day. Cities up and down the country had become overcrowded with people flocking for jobs that, despite the continued increase in manufacturing, were seriously oversubscribed, forcing them into homelessness, destitution and crime. Still, as the railways overtook canals as the focal point of that industrial revolution, so they opened up Britain for day trips and family holidays. Suddenly, the concept of fresh seaside air was affordable to everyone, quick kids, pack your buckets and spades. Mother Nature was now a mere few stations away, and galleries and museums were within reach of ordinary people.

In short, the world had grown smaller.

'Which canal is that, Mummy?' a small child asked, pressing his face to the glass as the train slowed into the station.

'That's not a canal, lovey.' The mother tousled the little boy's hair. 'That's the River Thames.'

Collecting her cases from the rack as they chugged to a halt, Julia thought, *this isn't just the River Thames. This is the start of my new life.*

# Chapter 28

'Good afternoon, is Clarice ready?' Julia flashed a lovely, broad, open smile at the maid, whose eye was almost knocked out by her pale blue leg o'mutton sleeve as she swept past. 'Two-thirty she told me, and you know how prompt my dear, darling friend is. Like clockwork that woman. In the parlour, is she?' Julia poked her head into the empty room as though she owned the place. 'No? Never mind, I'll wait for her here.'

'Er —'

'To err is human, to fetch your mistress is divine. Chop, chop!'

So far, so good. Julia had managed to barge her way into this elegant riverside mansion, with its twinkling chandeliers, carved panelled doors and rich, red papered walls peppered with paintings in ornate gold frames. Now she had about three minutes to come up with a decent bluff before that "dear, darling friend" sent her packing.

'Who the devil might you be?'

'Whitmore Photographic.' Julia handed over her visiting card with professional aplomb. 'Mr. Whitmore is looking to expand, and open a studio here in Bentley-on-Thames. I've been employed as his assistant for eight years, and he says if I drum up enough work, he'll let me run the shop myself. So I apologise for intruding on your grief, but if you'd like a photograph of your husband in his coffin, or perhaps seated in his favourite armchair, I can arrange that with the undertaker. It would be completely free of charge.'

'Would it now.' The woman's sharp green eyes looked Julia up and down, assessing her slashed blue silk, kitten heels and waist drawn in so tightly that Julia was convinced her kidneys and her lungs would be fused together permanently. She obviously passed muster, because far from throwing her out, Clarice motioned her to sit. 'I realise they're fashionable, but I'm not sure these momento mori pictures are in particularly good taste.'

'You'd prefer I took your portrait instead?'

'I will hang it above my late husband's desk. His loving wife, exactly as he remembers her, watching over him until we meet again.'

'Thank you. I can't tell you how much I appreciate your support.'

'Not at all. I admire any woman who carves a career for herself.'

'Taking matters into her own hands, to achieve her objective?'

'Exactly.'

'The same way you killed your husband, Mrs. Tate?'

'Oh, please, don't you start. I suppose that's why you picked me. You'd heard these ridiculous rumours, and looked for a famous name to kick off your little endeavour.'

'Well...' *Flutter, flutter* went Julia's lashes. 'There's this piece in the *Oakbourne Chronicle* that says your stepson thinks you did...'

The green eyes turned harder than Aaron Adelman's emeralds. 'They published that? I'll sue them. It's libel. I'll have that nasty little rag out of business before the end of the day — tch, I'm sorry, Mrs. McAllister. I shouldn't be venting my frustration on you. Of course you'd want a high profile name to pioneer your portfolio. I'd be more than happy to oblige.' Julia waited. 'Free of charge, you say?'

'Absolutely, and I'm sure you'd rather vent your frustration on your stepson, anyway.'

'The boy was far too attached to his father for comfort. Unnaturally so, in my opinion.'

'He was right, though, wasn't he. Why, when the window was broken, didn't your husband wake up?'

'This is really none of your business, but in the interest of justice and clearing these ridiculous smears, I'll tell you what I told Inspector Wylie of the Bentley police, when he asked the very same question. Dear Monty was an insomniac, which played havoc with his moods and digestion, and because of that, he regularly took laudanum, which put him into a deep slumber and often made him sleep in.'

'You don't think early morning is an odd time of day for a burglary?'

'Mrs. McAllister, I have no idea what isn't an odd time of day for a burglary. These things happen to other people, not us.'

'Unusual for the servants to be out, though? All of them at the same time?'

'It was Monday, for heaven's sake! This is when laundry needs to be sorted, shopping needs to be brought in, and the house cleaned top to bottom after the weekend. And as you can see, my dear, this is a big house.'

'Odd that the thief didn't clean the place out, though. He selected only the most valuable items, and yet the man caught fencing your husband's pocket watch and other personal pieces claimed he found them at the back, behind the wall.'

Clarice rolled her eyes. 'Well, he would say that, wouldn't he? I can't imagine many criminals actively seek a long stretch in a jail cell, so unless the thief confesses, I fear my husband's killer will walk free.'

'Highly unlikely, Mrs. Tate.'

'Listen, I can forgive my stepson. The father he worshipped was murdered in his bed, he is understandably upset. But I promise, if you start casting aspersions, I will sue you as well, and your silly little employer. I have a cast iron alibi for Monday morning. I was walking the streets of Bentley when my husband was killed.'

'Except you weren't. You never left this house.'

'Rubbish. At least fifty people saw me.'

'No. They saw Mary Mason walking the streets of Bentley when your husband was killed.' *She only has to look at you once, and you could walk down them stairs and before you got to the bottom step, she'll have you off pat. Walk, mannerisms, voice, the whole bleedin' works.* 'I don't know how long ago you decided to kill "dear Monty", but I know you went to great pains to create the perfect alibi. Let's see. You took the train to Oakbourne, because it's not too close, but not too far either, then what? Did you ask around for someone to audition in "your" theatre until you eventually found a failed actress, the same height and build as yourself? Or had you spotted the extra on stage beforehand, found out she was past her best but still desperate for limelight and fame, and would jump a chance to shine on Broadway?'

'I have no idea what you're talking about.'

'What did you promise her, Clarice? That if she could pass herself off as you, among people who knew you, fooling them all with your smile and your mannerisms in your clothes, the part would be hers, and her name would go up in lights?' Julia should have realised sooner. Why else would Mary Mason agree to meet someone at the theatre?

'Feel free to check my bank account, Mrs. McAllister. There have been no cash withdrawals.'

'Why would there be? This was about ambition, not money. Mary Mason used virtually every penny of her savings to buy herself a passage to New York, but instead of meeting you on

Monday afternoon at the Apollo, knowing she'd passed the audition with flying colours, and setting off to live her dream, you caved her head in. Twice to be exact, before you realised that modern hats are too well padded to crack a skull outright. So you pulled off the hat, finished her off, stripped her of the identical set of clothes you wore when you supposedly came home, only it's not easy, is it, moving a body? Still. You persevered, burying the evidence under a pile of bricks in the bushes, then calmly walked off, knowing you'd got away with it.'

'With what? Walking down the street? Having a deluded stepson, who can't accept facts any more than some jumped-up little photographer who thinks she's a reporter?'

'With the perfect murder, Clarice. Oh, come on. With half the servants out, the other half busy with mangles and dusters, and your husband drugged to the eyeballs, it was easy to break an obscure back window without anyone hearing, then bludgeon "dear Monty" to death while he slept.'

'This is a worse fantasy than that ridiculous newspaper. How come the servants didn't see me covered in blood?'

'You were naked when you killed him. Easy enough to wash yourself afterwards, then slip on the clothes "you" were seen in by oh-so-many people.'

'You have some nerve, coming into my house, accusing me of some hideous perversion!'

'I'm sure, if Inspector — what did you say his name was, Wylie? — conducted a search, they'd find the first Mrs. Tate's jewellery hidden away in your drawer. But the rest? The pocket watch, for instance. Pieces that were no good to you, but very obviously belonged to your husband? You stuffed them in a bag, threw them as far and as hard as you could, expecting one of the servants to find it, leading the police to conclude that the killer dropped it in his haste after you'd disturbed him by coming home.'

'Which is exactly what happened. The whole household heard me scream.'

'They heard you scream after Mary came in, before being ushered out the back without chance to change her clothes, but with a promise to meet up later to shore up that juicy role on Broadway.'

'I loved my husband —'

'I'm sure you did. Fat and bald — who wouldn't?'

Something changed in Clarice's emerald hard eyes. 'Very well. If you must know, he stank. Absolutely putrid. You can't imagine what it was like, forced to engage in all those intricate little bedroom games married couples are supposed to enjoy. He physically made me sick, Mrs. McAllister. The merest touch of his hand...' She shuddered with an authenticity that may or may not have been faked.

'No one forced you down the aisle.'

'He told me he was dying. When we met, he said he had just a few short months to live. If I married him, he said, if I could make him happy for those last few precious weeks, he'd change his will and leave everything to me instead of his son, and believe me, Monty didn't lack wealth. Even now I don't know if he lied to me or there was some miracle recovery, because, hand on heart, I worked bloody hard those first months to make him happy. But as time passed, he refused to discuss it and refused to change his will. He became autocratic, more demanding, until it reached the point where I couldn't stand the things he did to me any longer, so yes, I killed him. Good riddance, and it was a shame about the actress, but, honestly? That woman and her prime parted centuries ago, and

I was pretty sure, when I hired her as my double, that no one would miss her, and guess what? No one has.'

'She deserved better.'

'We all do, Mrs. McAllister — now why don't you take my portrait, it will add weight to the widow's show of grief, then get the hell out of here?'

'Aren't you worried I'll go to the police?'

'And say what? No one in their right mind confesses to premeditated murder, and since the gallows holds little appeal, no one but you will ever hear it.'

'Except me.' Benedict stepped out from behind the curtain.

'And me,' Orla said behind him.

'You little bitch,' Clarice hissed to Julia. 'Not that it matters a damn. The word of a deranged stepson, some bog Irish slut who can't keep her legs together, and the silly goose they duped into believing their story? That won't put a noose round my neck.'

'It won't,' Benedict agreed. 'But this will.' He pulled the other curtain aside. 'Inspector Wylie here very kindly allowed me to participate in this little game, so I could hear for myself what kind of woman you are. What kind of woman I've always known you to be.'

It had taken Dora to open Julia's eyes to just how cold the human heart could be. How it could fixate on greed and self-interest at the expense of everything, and everyone, else. And how women, in particular, were so adept at manipulating emotions.

Benedict Tate was indeed the gentlest of human souls that Orla believed him to be. It was his stepmother who had been using the magician's trick of illusion to pretend to be somebody else. Ben just happened to be the only one who saw through her.

# Chapter 29

Whenever Julia thought about catching the train, she never imagined it would be in the opposite direction to London. The opposite direction to Paris, Vienna, Niagara Falls, Tombstone. Or that her future would lie in the opposite direction, as well.

'What's this?' Collingwood asked, taking the envelope she handed him.

The sun was setting over the Common, turning the oaks, elms and birches to copper. Children wrapped in gloves and scarves scrambled to catch the leaves as they fell, or else kicked them into piles before diving in head first. Another week and Julia would be rubbing her hands in front of the fire, and that fire would not be in Egypt or New York or Rome. It would be right here, in her studio, because Collingwood was right, she couldn't give up on the victims she'd met.

*You can't change the past, but you can influence the future, JJ.*

Sam, the father she never had and the friend she most certainly did, was indeed wise, because what she hadn't understood, until yesterday, was just what he meant. By running, the past still controlled her. Only by facing down the enemy and standing her ground, could Julia hope to shape the future. A future that, like fingerprinting and mugshots, paved the way to building airtight cases through the medium of crime scene photography.

Finally, as Collingwood had oh-so-smugly pronounced, she understood. Every victim does matter. Good men or bad, their stories needed to be told, and if that story came to light quicker, and in sharper detail, through Julia's lens, and brought justice that much swifter, the world was a safer and far better place.

'This,' she replied, filling two glasses with cognac, 'is the difference between a narcissistic murderer walking the streets and your ensuring that she stays locked up for ever.'

Tomorrow was Alice's funeral. If Collingwood had had his way, he would have denied Emily attending, she'd be locked up already, but there were broader factors in play. The official line now was that she had inadvertently slipped her daughter too much laudanum, and while arsenic had been administered, it was in the misguided hope of orchestrating a cure. With Drs. Harrington and Poulson both testifying to this effect, there was no need for police involvement. Collingwood's superiors and fellow officers would be packing out the church tomorrow in support, wishing the bereaved parents nothing but well.

As for the asylum — poor Emily. She wouldn't be the first woman who'd gone mad with grief, shame, and self-reproach and had to be locked away, and the fact that it was an institution for the criminally insane implied that she'd tried to kill her husband and herself, so that they might join their only child and keep her company in Heaven.

Collingwood opened the envelope. 'Christ, there's £1,000 here!'

'£600 — don't exaggerate.'

'What's it for?'

'The new asylum for the criminally insane, just six miles away.' Julia had telephoned the superintendent and they'd spoken at length. 'If you're interested, they can admit your wife on Wednesday.'

'You know I am, but —'

'But nothing.' Hadn't he said it was imperative Emily didn't fool anyone inside the institution, especially the chaplain, into thinking she was cured? He couldn't keep tabs on her right the way over in Broadmoor. 'This covers the shortfall your police pay cannot.'

'Julia, no. I can't take this. I could never pay it back.'

'I'm not asking you to.'

The £600 she'd saved to start her new life would be better invested keeping cold-blooded killers where they belonged, stopping two fine officers from losing their jobs, keeping a damn good police station from closing, and opening the floodgates to hundreds of unnecessary and unwarranted appeals. The fact that it left Julia penniless and without a single item of cutlery, crockery or even furniture to her name was another matter. One crisis at a time, eh?

'What I do ask is that you never question, or look into, my past.'

Collingwood leaned his runner's frame back in the chair and looped one arm over the side. For several minutes his grey eyes bored into hers.

She didn't blink.

'Bribing a police officer is a serious offence.'

'A girl would need to have committed a crime to do that.'

'Hm.' He picked up the glass and warmed it in his hand. Julia's heart stopped pumping. 'My counterpart from Bentley telephoned. Inspector Wylie. He said my police photographer did sterling work in bringing an ice-cold killer to book.'

'The person to thank is Orla Keane. That ice-cold killer would have walked free, had it not been for her.' It was a slight exaggeration, but it was the best Julia could do. 'So it wouldn't hurt you or Charlie Kincaid to give her a scoop now and then, in return for her keeping you informed on cases that cross jurisdictions? You'll find her surprisingly ethical.'

'Ethics. Exactly. Happy as I am that the case is closed on Mary Mason, my point is, I didn't join the police to give free passes for crimes.'

Julia could see her mother's bloodied, swollen face running with tears. Her brother's spine, twisted from the beating. The look of surprise on her stepfather's face, when the first bullet ripped into his chest. 'This is me, John. No more, no less, no apologies.'

Collingwood swirled the cognac round in the glass, watching the last rays of light play on the crystal. 'Judging people by their actions not their past is the prosecution's job, not mine. This money is wrong, you and I both know it.' Suddenly, there was an empty hole where Julia's heart used to be. So much for life on her terms, not the Devil's. 'It's not just illegal, it's wholly unethical, but you, Mrs. McAllister.' Collingwood drained his glass in one swallow. 'Have got yourself a deal.'

# A NOTE TO THE READER

Well, Reader —

If you enjoyed *Cast Iron*, I'd very much value your review on **Amazon** and **Goodreads**. And to find out more about what I'm working on next, find me at **Facebook (Marilyn Todd–Crime Writer)**.

Marilyn Todd.

**www.marilyntodd.com**

**Sapere Books** is an exciting new publisher of brilliant fiction and popular history.

To find out more about our latest releases and our monthly bargain books visit our website: **saperebooks.com**

Printed in Great Britain
by Amazon

39892254R00131